SAM CRESCENT AND STACEY ESPINO

EVERNIGHT PUBLISHING ®

www.evernightpublishing.com

Copyright© 2019

Sam Crescent and Stacey Espino

Editor: Karyn White

Cover Artist: Jay Aheer

ISBN: 978-0-3695-0109-7

ALL RIGHTS RESERVED

SAM CRESCENT AND STACEY ESPINO

#

Breeding Season, 3

Sam Crescent and Stacey Espino

Copyright © 2018

⚜ ◆ ◆ ◆ ⚜

Chapter One

"Her stomach looks so cute," said Jake. He was swooning over his pregnant mate, and Liam was fucking sick of hearing about it.

"Keep that shit to yourself," he said.

Jake glared at him. "You're even bitchier than usual. What's going on with you?"

Liam had just turned fifty. He was the alpha of his pack and was still without a woman to call his own. He could hardly sleep nights knowing he still didn't have an heir to take over his place in the pack once he was too old to reign.

"Cabin fever," he said.

"We're almost finished construction. Don't worry, we'll be out of your hair within the week."

"Just hurry it up."

He stood and stretched out his muscles. Since three of his packmates had found their mates within the last year, he wanted all the happy couples out of the main cabin. They owned thousands of acres of untouched forest, with a small settlement for their pack. Lately, he'd been sleeping in his fur in their old wolf den rather than his comfortable king-sized bed. Listening to Jake, Eli, and Ben fucking in the next rooms had put him in a perpetual black mood.

Why were the gods forsaking him? He'd been searching for his mate for decades, but all he'd found were one-night stands. Liam began to trek away from the camp. His spirits were down, and tonight he'd drown his misery in cheap whisky.

"Come on," he called to his dog, Alphie. The German shepherd ran up beside him, tagging along. He'd always loved dogs, and the fact had made him a pariah of sorts. Shifters believed dogs were lesser beings and couldn't understand why he'd want one as a pet. He blamed his human side. Regardless, everyone knew to keep their paws off Alphie, even in their wolf form, or they'd deal with him.

The forest was quiet at this time of evening, just the remnants of the sunset between the leaves above. He loved this land, but the loneliness was driving him insane. He wanted what many of his friends had, a mate, love, happiness, and regular sex. As a shifter, his sexual drive was off the charts, and he was tired of cheap women and random hookups. He wanted to devote himself to one woman, but it had to be the one chosen for him. Maybe he'd die alone, his legacy ending along with him.

Liam had a love-hate relationship with humankind. He used to work as a driver for the local lumber camp, but as alpha he preferred to stay on the land, ensuring it was safe. Most of his pack had outside jobs during the day, but at night they patrolled their territory in shifts. They had enemies that would be eager to claim their property, and there was no way he'd let that happen. It was survival of the fittest in their world.

He rarely ventured into the small town. The gossipy humans served to piss him off, and he wouldn't feed their craving for information. After years of his refusing to warm up to them, they now kept their distance—exactly how he liked it. Their identities as shifters was a carefully guarded secret, and since many humans in the small northern town liked to hunt, that didn't put them on common ground. Zealous hunters often targeted wolves.

The grocery store was a beacon of light as he emerged from the forest. He rolled out his shoulders. He'd get what he needed and have a full-blown pity party. He hoped his mood would improve once he had the main cabin to himself again.

He ran a hand through his hair. This would be a quick stop. His boots crunched along the gravel before he stepped onto the paved parking area. A couple streetlamps highlighted the nearly empty lot. He knew the navy pickup belonged to the cashier, and the guy stocking shelves owned the red Honda. The manager was a loud bitch, but she was only in during the day.

As he neared the front doors, an unusual scent caught his attention. It made his fangs prick his gums. He resisted his urge to shift and investigate. He'd come to the store for his booze, and he planned to get it. Liam didn't trust his own instincts at this point, not with his black mood.

Alphie sensed his unease, barking into the darkness. "Relax, boy. I'll just be a minute." He left his dog outside and entered the grocery store.

The bright florescent lights irritated his eyes once he entered. As a shifter, all his senses were magnified.

He grabbed a basket and began his search. Often, he ate in his wolf form—rabbit, deer, whatever he decided to hunt. Sometimes he'd save what he caught and barbeque it at their camp, human-style. That's why he liked to have hot sauce on hand.

As he entered the first aisle, the cashier monitored his every move. Did she think he was there to steal? He ground his teeth, tempted to tell her to "fuck off". Instead, he made his way through the store, collecting what he needed.

He still couldn't get that scent off his mind. It was even stronger inside the store, perfuming the air to the point of distraction. It was delicious, a sweet vanilla that made his cock hard. He nearly laughed out loud. Having blue balls for months had made him delirious.

As he turned the corner into the produce aisle, he saw her. She was a vision, long red hair twirled up on top her head, and big green eyes. He watched her move, putting things into her basket without paying attention to her surroundings. She was the essence of a woman, with lush curves and pouty lips—and she was, without a doubt, the source of the scent.

He practically drooled as he envisioned stripping her naked and eating her until she came on his tongue. He licked his lips. Gods, he wanted her, and he *would* have her. Never in his life had he felt such a strong pull.

The sudden realization finally struck him, nearly bringing him to his knees. She was his mate. Could it actually be true? Was she the one sent by the gods? She was human, but at this point in his life, he didn't give a fuck. She was gorgeous, a ray of sunshine to his darkness.

He watched her for the longest time, frozen in place at the end of the aisle. Where had she come from? Maybe dropped right out of heaven. He'd never seen her before, and he sure as hell had never noticed that addictive scent before. She had rounded hips, perfect for child-bearing. He could already imagine her ripe with their child, with his heir. Her tits were huge, barely contained under her beige canvas jacket. Liam had never wanted a woman more.

****

Rebecca wasn't a people person.

Shopping at the local grocery store each week was a necessary evil. She came an hour before closing when she knew it would be empty, and the sun had set, so no prying eyes could stare at her in the parking lot.

She'd moved to the micro-town five months ago. City life was too hectic, and her therapist recommended somewhere with a slower pace. Since her editing job was an online position, she had the flexibility to pack up and move anywhere in the world. She'd stopped taking her anxiety meds in exchange for the endless miles of evergreens beyond her apartment windows. The fresh air, the quiet, it had all done wonders for her peace of mind.

The townsfolk were a different story. They loved to stare, even point, probably because she was new and hardly ventured outside. At least in the city she had anonymity.

Rebecca pulled her grocery list from her front pocket and glanced at her notes. The soft elevator music relaxed her. She needed the essentials and some fruit and vegetables. Since moving up north, she'd also vowed to start eating healthier.

She wandered up the produce aisle, glancing at the selection. Rebecca tried to imagine the meals she could make. They had fresh asparagus today, so she splurged and added it to her basket. Carrots, mini-potatoes, and Brussel sprouts would be nice sautéed in a sauce pan. She was so focused on her task that she bumped into a person.

She gasped, horrified. There hadn't been anyone in sight before she started looking at the vegetables. "I'm so sorry," she said. She set down her basket.

The man took a step back and narrowed his eyes as he looked her up and down. Yes, she had a lot of weight left to lose, but he didn't have to be obvious about it. "I've never seen you before."

"I'm new to town. Well, kind of new. I've only been here for five months."

He smirked, a dimple appearing on his cheek.

"What's your name?"

"Rebecca."

He glanced at her basket. "You like vegetables?"

"They're healthy," she said. "I'll Google a good way to cook them up."

"Google?"

She paused. Was he joking?

"I don't come to town too often." The man held out his basket. "But I do like to indulge myself once in a while." He winked. There was a bottle of hot sauce, a bag of limes, and two bottles of whisky.

Rebecca cocked her head to the side. "No veggies?"

"There's enough plant life in the forest. Trust me, I don't want any more."

The guy was a good foot taller than she was. He wore a light jacket, but the t-shirt underneath pulled taut over a hard body. In all the months she'd been in her new town, he was the first guy worth looking at. His stubble was coming in thick, and his eyes were dark and hypnotic. If she'd seen him before, she definitely would have remembered.

"Well, I'm sorry for bumping you. You're okay, right?"

"More than okay."

Why hadn't he moved? He kept staring at her like he recognized her or something. Her instincts told her to keep talking, to flirt with the stranger. The devil on her other shoulder reminded her that she was socially awkward, destined to live out her life alone. As usual, she sided with her negative thoughts and kept walking away from him.

Life in her new apartment consisted of sitting behind a screen most of the time. She edited books and articles by day and read romance novels by night. By now she should be looking for her own happily ever after, but dating required socialization. Since she rarely left her home, and wasn't interested in social gatherings, she was shit out of luck. Internet dating didn't interest her, even if she could hide behind her computer.

After she paid for her food, collected her bags, and walked to the exit, she hated herself more than ever. Why couldn't she take a risk for once? She was too afraid of rejection and disappointment to the point she'd never find a man.

Her eyes adjusted to the minimal lighting outside as she lugged her four bags. She didn't like to drive, and the walk wasn't too far. There were two pickup trucks in the parking lot that weren't there when she'd come earlier. The engines were running, the headlights highlighting a group of men. She hoped she'd be able to slip by on the path undetected.

"Hey, what you got there?"

Rebecca prayed they weren't talking to her. She hoped she was hidden by shadows.

"Hey, sugar tits, come over here."

She picked up the pace, her heart racing like a freight train. When an arm wrapped around her from behind before she could escape the parking lot, she screamed and dropped her bags. Another man took her bags to the bed of his pickup truck and started rooting through the contents.

"Nothing interesting here," the man said. He tossed her asparagus, baby potatoes rolling out in several directions. Tears burned her eyes as she struggled against the man holding her.

"Stop it," she shouted. "Leave me alone."

"Why, baby? The night is young," said the man holding her.

Is this actually happening to me? The townsfolk could be creepy, but they weren't criminals. She'd never seen these men before and wasn't sure what their plans were for her. Were they going to rape her? Would someone from inside the store hear her screams?

"Hands off."

The arm pinned around her chest loosened slightly. It gave her enough room to struggle free. They turned to the voice at once. It was the stranger from the grocery store. Mr. Tall, Dark, and Handsome. She felt relieved and guilty because he'd never be able to protect her from six guys.

He had a German shepherd, and its fangs were bared. Maybe the dog would scare them off.

"We're just having a little fun here. Why don't you back off?" said one of the men. The guys from the truck closed in on them.

"You can have all the fucking fun you want, boys. But not with her."

No one had ever stuck up for her, and her heart swelled watching her knight in shining armor risk life and limb for her. She didn't even know his name, because she'd been too scared to ask.

"Give us your bags, hotshot. Then leave while you can."

She stood frozen in place, unwilling to save herself and leave him to fend for himself. Rebecca hoped for a miracle.

"I won't be giving you anything. Of course, you can always try to take my bags," he said.

Why was he antagonizing them? She could smell the alcohol coming from the men, and they were big and burly bushmen.

"Yeah, that's a real good idea." The man who'd been holding her a minute ago, walked toward the stranger and his dog. The shepherd began barking and growling, but his owner told him to settle.

As soon as the guy reached for the grocery bag, her mystery man gave him a short, quick jab to the face with his free hand. The impact must have been intense because he fell over, unconscious, like a tree toppling in the forest.

"What the hell?" said one of the other men.

"Alphie, watch my bag, eh?" The stranger set his groceries down beside his dog, who was now sitting obediently, albeit not happy with the conflict.

She watched in horror, waiting for the remaining five men to beat the stranger senseless. Instead, he moved like a skilled mercenary, taking them out one by one. She swore he hadn't even put effort into his attack, looking bored but pissed off.

Within seconds, all the men were on the ground in various states of injury. Some groaned and cried out; others were knocked out. Her stranger adjusted his jacket, then returned to collect his bag and his dog. She still hadn't moved.

"Rebecca, are you okay?"

"H-how do you know my name?" Her anxiety was through the damn roof, and it didn't help that she no longer took any medications to calm her down. She was determined to live a more natural, healthy life.

He smirked. "You told me in the grocery store, remember? My name's Liam, by the way." One of the men attempted to sit up, and Liam kicked him in the chest.

"I don't know what to say."

"You look a little pale. I should walk you home." He glanced over at her bags. Her groceries were strewn all over the truck bed and parking lot. Liam frowned.

"Thank you," she said. "I don't know what I would have done without you."

He shrugged. "Deer season opens this Saturday, so the weekend warriors will be flocking to town. Most of them are assholes, so you should be on guard the next couple weeks."

"I never knew."

He hooked his arm around hers and helped her up the path to the street. She was still in shock. They walked along the side of the road towards her apartment. It was a small triplex that used to be a century home. She had the loft, and she loved the views from her windows even if it was small.

"So, Rebecca, tell me about yourself," he said.

She decided not to let her fears control her this time. She'd been given a round two with the same man. "I'm an editor. I work from home." Oh God, that was about it. Her life sounded more pathetic than it seemed.

"I love to read. Guess we have something in common."

The three of them continued along, the road getting darker as they grew more distant from the lights in the parking lot. "Why didn't you let your dog help you out back there? Not that you needed it."

He smiled. "I didn't want him to get hurt."

Was it possible to fall in love in less than an

hour?

"I love animals," she said. "Dogs, cats, rabbits, you name it."

Liam stopped, turning her to face him. "We're a lot alike, you and I. What about wolves, Rebecca? Do you like them?"

"I love wolves," she said. "They're so beautiful and feral. Of course, I wouldn't like to meet one on the way home." She giggled, then stopped herself.

"You have nothing to worry about," he said. Liam trailed his finger along the edge of her jaw, a feather-light touch. The way he looked at her made butterflies flutter in her stomach. "I'll protect you from the wolves, too."

Rebecca might be a thirty-year-old virgin, but she could envision changing all that for a man like him. "I bet you could."

They began walking again, their hands occasionally brushing, bringing her body to life. The crickets droned all around them, a soothing melody. She was surprised how comfortable she felt around this man. New people usually made her clam up.

When they reached her home, they stopped in front. A lamp she'd left on glowed from the third-floor window. The faint scent of his woodsy cologne had her breathing in deeply for more. "Who's waiting for you?" he asked. "Are you married?"

She shook her head. "I live alone."

"You're new to town. You'll have to let me show you around one day."

Rebecca felt a jolt of excitement. This gorgeous, beast of a man was actually interested in her? Or was he just being nice?

Chapter Two

"You're different," Ben said.

Liam glanced toward his friend and shook his head. "No, I'm not."

"Yeah, you are. Since you came back home the other night, you've been ... happy."

Of course he was happy. Rebecca had given him something to think about other than his lack of a mate, or the fact he was desperate to meet the right woman. Rebecca called to him in a way no other woman had. He felt possessive, fueled by desire and a need to get to know her. She was perfect for him in every single way. He knew it deep down into his soul, and there was no way that was ever going to change.

Since meeting her, every second that he thought about her, he couldn't get the image of her heavily pregnant with his child out of his mind. She was his mate, he was sure of it. The scent of her, the need to take care of her, it all led to one conclusion—Rebecca, the mystery shopping lady, was his mate.

"What's wrong with me being happy? I'm not moody or snapping. All of you have been complaining about it."

"You've met a woman, haven't you?" Ben asked.

"I've met someone, yes. No, I'm not telling you about her or anything else. Just know that it's serious."

"Come on, you can't do that. There's no way you can leave us hanging like this," Ben said. "I'll tell the others."

Liam smirked. "Go ahead, tell the others. I thought your places would be ready by now."

"We've hit a couple of snags."

"You mean your mates want it a certain way and now you're having to wait to make the necessary changes," Liam said, aware of his fellow packmates' plans. His friends couldn't say no to their females, and it was no surprise. He saw their daily devotion to each other. It was just another reason why he wanted to go out tonight.

Coffee wasn't something he really enjoyed, but the chance to see Rebecca again was too hard to pass up. Besides, they were heading to a place that had seats outside, and he didn't like being in buildings, especially with humans. The scent of them often annoyed and irritated him, driving his wolf crazy. She wanted him to bring Alphie as well.

"When you're mated you'll understand. We all want them to be happy and to give them whatever their hearts desire," Ben said.

Liam smiled. "I get it. I do."

"You know, I think I like crazy, brooding Liam a lot more. I'm used to him. Are you getting laid?"

He sighed. "Look, I've got a date, and I like this woman."

"Who is it?"

"You don't know her."

"She's not part of the pack?"

"Nope."

"A casual hookup?"

He snarled, hating the thought of any man considering Rebecca a casual thing.

Whoa, down, boy!

"Wow, I've never known you to have a reaction like that. Are you okay?" Ben asked.

"I don't know, but until we know exactly what is going on, don't refer to Rebecca as anything other than her name." He'd been known these past fifty years to be in complete control. Even as a young one, his wolf had never taken control of him.

He'd been one of the few wolves within the pack that showed zero emotion, and his wolf constantly stayed at bay until he needed him.

This was the first time that he hadn't been in control.

"Are you sure having coffee is a good idea?"

"I think so. I want some coffee."

"You hate coffee," Ben said.

Liam was fast growing bored with his best friend. He wasn't used to feeling so fucking desperate to get out of his home. This was his sanctuary.

"Could you stop with the third degree already? And for the record, the dining room table is for eating on, not for fucking your woman."

He saw Ben's cheeks heat.

"I've seen way too much of your, Eli's, and Jake's asses. That table is for when *I* have a mate so that I can fuck her on it, not you, not your mates, mine. Now, do you think you can stick to your bedrooms tonight?"

He didn't give Ben time to answer. Leaving his home, he whistled for Alphie, and smiled as his dog trotted toward him. He really did love this guy.

"You ready to go and meet our girl?" he asked.

Alphie cocked his head to the side.

"Yeah, you understand me, don't you? Always could." He kissed the top of his dog's head. "I could really use the walk, but I know that's going to look weird. Especially when I bring her back here one day. Don't want to freak her out too much just yet. We're taking the jeep." Alphie whined. "I know, boy. I know. I want to walk, too. We've got to look a little normal to my female. Don't want her thinking I'm a bit weird before we've even got there. Now, remember, if it looks like I'm screwing up, you've got to do that adorable thing. Remember, roll over, show your belly."

He laughed as Alphie did just that. "Good boy. Come on then, let's go."

Whistling to himself, he made his way over to his jeep, opened the door, and waited for Alphie to climb up before jumping in himself. He rarely used the jeep as he preferred to walk in the open forest, to enjoy the nature surrounding him.

Being in a metal can didn't exactly help ease any of his anxiety. Starting up his jeep, he put it in reverse, and followed the main path away from the house, moving toward the dirt path that would lead him to the main road.

Once on the road, he lowered the window down, and inhaled the fresh air that was invaded by the fumes of the car. This was another reason he hated the damn car.

"Enough with the miserable talk. Get over your shit. Come on, she doesn't want to meet brooding Liam."

Before they had parted the other night, Rebecca had given him her phone number, and he'd done the same. He'd been staring at his phone all day, wanting to make a date with her but worried that he'd be screwing it up, or doing something that wasn't conventional. In his world, the men chased after the women, but after seeing a few modern-day movies, he'd discovered that the women of the world liked to chase after men.

He didn't like it, not one bit, but he was willing to try it.

So, when Rebecca had called, he'd been fucking ecstatic.

Pushing his foot on the gas, he checked the time and saw that he was going to be twenty minutes early. He didn't mind being early. It would give him time to think, to get accustomed to his surroundings. As he pulled into the small town, he saw the sign for the coffee shop where she wanted to meet. There was a parking bay across from the shop, and he stopped the jeep in one of the spots. Alphie jumped out, and together they crossed the empty road. The scent of vanilla filled his senses, and there she sat, her cell phone between her fingers.

She hadn't spotted him yet, and he got the chance to simply take her all in. Her beauty, her everything. The other night hadn't been long enough.

Alphie chose that moment to bark, drawing her attention. The moment she saw Liam, her smile did something to him. His wolf pounced against the tight cage he kept him in.

Ours!
Take her!
Breed her!
She's ready!

The scent of her fertility was heavy in the air, and his cock hardened at the smell. She truly was an intoxicating female.

"You came," she said.

He heard the edge to her voice, and he didn't like it.

"You didn't think I would?"

"I don't know. I … I stared at my cell for, like, two days wanting to call you. I'm not this kind of woman. I mean, I'm not forward. I know we've only just met and you're probably already married or have a ton of girlfriends or whatever, and I really wanted to get coffee with you. Not that I think I'm good girlfriend material, and could you please stop me now while I'm babbling?"

"I kind of like you babbling."

"I don't. I'm sorry. I'm so nervous."

"How about we sit?" He nodded toward the chairs, and she smiled.

"Thank you. I was worried that I'd frightened you

away."

"I was going to call you for coffee," he said.

"You were?"

"Yes. I didn't want to seem too ... desperate."

She winced. "Did I sound desperate?"

"No, no, not at all. It's just when we want a female, I mean woman, erm, I come from a pack, a family, I mean, that er, we're the ones that chase the women."

She frowned at him. "I find it quite refreshing how you talk. It's, like ... strange but not."

****

Rebecca didn't know what it was about this man, but she couldn't stop thinking about him. He'd saved her the other night when no one else could have, and he did so without even allowing his dog to get hurt.

"I see you brought Alphie." The dog came to her wagging his tale as he did. "He's so cute."

Liam lowered himself down into one of the chairs, and she was surprised it took his size.

"My dog comes everywhere with me."

"It's why I suggested this place. They allow for pets and dogs. There's even a little dog bowl for water."

"Go on, boy, go drink."

She watched the dog go and drink some water before coming back and sitting beside his master.

Pushing some hair off her forehead, she smiled at him. "So, I wanted to thank you for the other night."

"You don't even have to mention it. It's never normally like that here, at least not from what I've seen."

"How do you mean?"

"Not all men behave that way in front of a lady."

She glanced down at the table. The menu was beneath a coaster, and she picked it up. "Tell me what you'd like and I'll go and order it."

They only offered a small selection of sandwiches and nibbles.

Deciding what she wanted, she was about to ask him why he'd been staring at her, his menu untouched.

"You pick something for me."

"You don't have any allergies?"

"None."

"Anything you don't like?" she asked.

"I'll like whatever you pick."

"Oh, okay." She got up and made her way inside. The waitress took her order and promised to bring it outside when she was done.

Rebecca's nerves were getting to her again. She hated being out in public. It's why she'd made a life for herself working over the Internet. No one had to see their editor in this new world of e-books.

It's fine.

He's not like anyone else.

Liam was still waiting, fussing with his dog as she sat back down.

She loved watching him with Alphie. It seemed so right the two of them together. Dog was after all man's best friend.

"They'll be out in a few minutes."

"Do you have any pets yourself?" he asked.

"None at the moment. I've been working on getting my company up and running, and it's been a full-time commitment."

"I imagine being an editor is pretty intense."

"Oh, believe me it can be. Everyone seems to think they're an editor these days."

"I'll take your word for it."

"What is it you do?"

He opened his mouth to answer, but the waitress came out.

Rebecca tried not to show how overwhelmed she was by the scent of the woman's perfume. She was also thrusting her chest out, trying to catch Liam's eye.

Mortified, Rebecca didn't know where to look but found herself looking at Liam. The disgust on his face was clear to see. He didn't want the woman's flirting, and seeing that, she felt happier.

"I'm sorry about that," Liam said after the waitress left.

"Don't worry about it. You're a good-looking guy." Realizing what she said, her cheeks heated. "I mean, of course she'd want to flirt with you."

"You think I'm good looking?" he asked. The smile he flashed her way should be illegal. Her panties went wet, and arousal flooded her body. She wanted him, and she'd never had such a strong and instant reaction before in her life.

A growl filled the air.

The strangest thing of all was she didn't believe it came from his dog.

Tension seemed to grow, and she waited, sure that he'd been the one to growl at her like that. Why wasn't she afraid?

With Liam, she knew she was safe.

"You know you're good looking." She charged the subject. "So, you've lived here all your life?"

"Yes."

"Do the rumors bother you?"

"Rumors?"

"You know, about the wolves." She'd heard the local gossip and myths about a pack of wolves that lived out in the forest. She loved wolves so much, not that she'd ever seen one herself.

"What about them?" Liam asked.

"You've lived here. You know, the rumor that

men can change into them, or that they eat humans, or steal women to take to their lair."

"Wow, they're still talking about that shit?"

Again, his speech seemed to completely confuse her. "Still? How old are you?" she asked.

"I mean, my dad talked about them, you know. That's what I meant."

"I'm thirty years old, just so you know," she said.

"I'm around the same age."

He didn't sound so sure, but she decided to let it go. As far as dates went, this one was going a little strangely, and she didn't know if that was because of her, or if she just wasn't used to going on dates all that much.

Being a busy recluse didn't exactly leave much time in the way of a social life. They finished their sandwiches and drinks. All the time she couldn't stop laughing as Alphie kept jumping up against the table.

After their food was gone, and silence fell between them, Rebecca didn't want the moment to end.

"So, I was thinking, if it's not too forward, would you like to show me around sometime? I know this place has a lot of rich history, with settlers dating back a couple of hundred years ago. I'd love to know more, if you'd be willing?"

"I would love to. If you want, I can take you to a few places tonight. The night is still young."

Part of her wanted to jump at the chance. Another was nervous about getting home. She didn't want to be out too late.

Live dangerously.

Liam was a hot, sexy man, and she wanted to spend time with him.

"I'd love to."

"We'll have to take my car."

"Of course."

He whistled to Alphie, and she followed him as he walked toward a jeep. He opened the passenger door, and she burst out laughing as Alphie nudged her out of the way.

"I guess he wants to be in first."

"He's adorable. You've got a keeper there."

"I think I'll keep him. He's good company."

He held his hand out, and she took it, climbing into his jeep.

Tonight, she would live a little recklessly. She'd never done anything like this before in her life. Putting her bag on the floor, she sat back as he pulled out of the parking spot. He spun the jeep around, and they were heading back out of the town.

"Where are you taking me?" she asked.

"It's a secluded spot, one of my favorites. It's near a lake. A lot of high school kids are there now as it's a make-out spot."

She'd never been to a make-out spot before. Alphie butted his head on her knee, and she stroked behind his ears. She couldn't resist glancing toward the man in the driver's seat. His strong arms caught her attention. They were thick, strong, and corded with muscle. No wonder the men who'd attacked her didn't stand a chance against him.

He was the strongest man she'd ever seen before in her life, tall as well. She'd always been a sucker for big men.

"Did that waitress leave you her phone number?" she asked.

"I tossed it in the trash. I wasn't there to pick up that woman, Rebecca. I answered your call. No one else's."

She thought she'd seen the woman's number on a napkin, and she'd been gutted. Now of course, she liked

Liam. He was truly different.

There's no way Rebecca could have met him on a dating site. She'd attempted them a few years back and hadn't found any luck with them. A couple of the men had even been married and only used the sites to have affairs.

Liam pulled up into a parking space. "We're here."

The area was deserted, and she didn't see any signpost to say where they were.

He was at her door as she opened it, helping her out. "You can leave your bag. No one will touch my jeep."

Listening to him, she felt that electric thrill rush through her body as he kept hold of her hand, leading her down a dirt path. The bushes and trees were overgrown, but the path was clear from many years of use.

If kids truly made out here, she understood it. The air felt so calm, so peaceful. This had to be the single craziest thing she'd ever done.

Liam was a stranger to her.

She didn't know him at all.

He'd protected her, and rather than fight it, she embraced everything. Pushing all of her negative thoughts to one side, she focused on Liam and the path he was leading her down.

This felt right.

Liam stopped at the clearing, and she gasped. There was light from the crescent moon and stars reflected off the surface of the lake.

It truly was breathtaking, beautiful, and as Liam pulled her into his arms, everything felt exactly as it should be.

Chapter Three

Everything had been going better than he expected—until he sensed one of his rivals nearby. He'd recognize their stench anywhere. The lake was neutral ground, so neither of them were trespassing on the other's territory. But his alpha wolf didn't want a rival pack member near his mate.

"I could stay here all night," she said, oblivious to the potential danger. Rebecca was mesmerized by the moon and stars. The water was nearly as still as glass tonight, the air comfortably warm. Although he'd never had a serious relationship, he knew how human females liked to be treated by a man. They wanted romance and attention, and he'd give her more than she could handle.

"Anytime you want to come, just let me know. People hike around here in the day, but I like it best at night."

"You're right. I've never seen anything like this."

"There are a lot of other beautiful spots around the town. I'll show them all to you." He dared to tuck her hair behind her ear. She didn't flinch away, which was a good sign. Liam felt a strand between his fingers for a few moments. "I've never seen this color before."

"I'm cursed. It must be my Irish roots."

"It's stunning, Rebecca. Reminds me of the harvest moon."

Her mouth parted slightly, and she looked up at him with those big green eyes. She was shy with men, maybe uncomfortable with compliments, but right now he could feel her desire.

A wolf bayed in the distance, and she pressed her body against his, her forearms on his chest. He could barely contain his low growl of satisfaction. She'd sought him for comfort, and his little human had no idea how far he'd go to protect her.

He owned the night.

Liam was alpha to one of the most lethal wolf shifter packs in the state. Everyone in his world knew not to mess with the Grey Valley Pack. The human world saw a reclusive group of men who lived off the grid. They had no idea what Liam was capable of.

"I thought you liked wolves," he said. He used a finger to gently tilt her chin up. She kept close, her big juicy tits pressed against his chest.

"I love them, but I don't think they'd love me. We're so deep in the forest. They could attack us."

He wrapped his arms around the small of her back, loving their closeness. "I know a few wolves that would love you," he said. "And as long as you're with me, you have nothing to worry about."

"You're my knight in shining armor, aren't you? You saved me from those jerks and you're ready to protect me from the wolves."

He leaned down, picking up on her lead. Liam kissed her on the lips, softly, tentatively. She grabbed fistfuls of his shirt, pushing up on her toes so they could kiss deeper. She tasted delicious. He explored her with his tongue, her mewling sounds spurring him on. Liam kissed along her jawline to her neck. His fangs pricked his gumline, his humanity starting to slip away.

"I'll do anything for you," he said.

She tossed her head back as he suckled her pulse. "You barely know me."

"That's why I'm trying my best to change that. I want you to be mine, Rebecca. You won't regret choosing me."

Instead of being insulted, she reached her arms around his shoulders, her fingers combing into the hair at the base of his head. His eyes rolled back. Could she feel the hard ridge of his cock pushing against her stomach? If she could, it hadn't turned her off. "I'm not sure what you're saying, Liam. Are you asking me to be your girlfriend?"

"I don't want a girlfriend," he said. "I want a woman, a mate, you."

"Me?"

He nodded, then kissed her on the lips again.

"How many women have you said that to?"

Liam frowned. "Only you. Don't you believe in fate, Rebecca?"

"I never really thought about it," she said.

He wondered how many men she'd had. It didn't matter, because he'd be the only one from this day forward. "Have you never been in love?"

She shied away a bit. "I'm not very good with people, Liam. This is all new for me. I just feel comfortable around you for some reason."

"That's a good thing, baby." He ran a hand through her hair. "Are you telling me you've never been in a serious relationship?"

Rebecca bit her lip. "I've had issues with ... anxiety. I'm not good with social situations. That's the main reason I moved out here. I don't want to be on medication, so I decided to trade it for some fresh air, peace, and quiet."

His wolf didn't give a shit about anxiety. Rebecca was a virgin, untouched by other men. The knowledge excited him, his claim even stronger. She'd be his. Only his. He couldn't wait to eat her sweet virgin pussy.

"You're good with me."

She drew patterns at the side of his neck with her fingertips. It was an unconscious act, but it was driving him crazy. She had no idea the power she held over him.

"It's strange, I know. There's something different

about you. You're not like other men."

"Not at all."

Alphie started barking at the wall of dark forest behind them. Liam had been so engrossed in everything Rebecca that he hadn't paid attention to his surroundings. Now that he took notice, he could smell the pungent scent of alcohol. Kids came to drink and make out, so he wasn't threatened until two men came out from between the trees. Only they weren't men at all.

They were shifters, but not from the rival Silverback Warrior Pack. They were dressed in camo, so they were likely playing human, coming out for hunting season. Over time, many werewolves swapped feral life for easy human living. They gave up shifting for so long, they could barely call themselves wolves at all. Their senses and instincts got rusty without use, so they may not even realize what he was. For some reason, Rebecca was a damn magnet for trouble. He had a feeling these urban shifters were pulled to his mate since he hadn't marked her yet. That would have to be remedied soon. There was no way he'd let anything happen to her.

"Can I help you, boys?" he asked. This was his alone time with Rebecca, and he didn't want things interrupted.

"You're trespassing," said the blond.

"Actually, we're not. It's public land. And I'd like to enjoy a nice evening with my woman, if you don't mind."

The blond scoffed. "You think you're a tough guy, don't you? I can take your woman, and you wouldn't be able to do a fucking thing about it."

"What did you say?" He shifted Rebecca behind the wall of his body.

"I said you're a pussy."

Liam cracked his neck to the side, his alpha

power making his muscles tense. "I get that you're both wasted, but when you threaten my mate, we have a big fucking problem."

"It's okay, Liam. Let's just go," Rebecca whispered behind him.

"Listen to her," said his dark-haired friend. "Or we might keep her for ourselves."

"Take her," said Liam. "I fucking dare you."

Rebecca clutched his shirt from behind.

Liam flashed his fangs, his eyes morphing into wolven yellow. He'd told Rebecca they lived in a decent town, but this was the second time he'd had to kick ass in front of her. He hoped this shit was earning him some boyfriend points.

The two hunters turned to look at each other. "Shit," the blond whispered. The realization of what they were dealing with was starting to sink in past their alcoholic stupor. The dark-haired one backed off, the blond still holding his ground. Liam rushed forward, punching the blond square in the face. He'd held back, but the man still toppled down on his ass. It wasn't enough. He needed to put the fear of the devil in these pricks, a warning to never threaten his woman again. After grabbing the guy's collar and lifting him up, he used his free right hand to punch him a couple more times. This time he was out cold.

"Don't forget your friend," he called out into the darkness. The other man was long gone.

****

This couldn't be good for her anxiety.

Then why did it turn her on? She was a sick puppy if she enjoyed watching Liam punch a man into unconsciousness—and she did enjoy every moment of it. He made her feel safe, invincible. His shirt pulled tight across his back when he bent over to hit that bully, all his hard muscles flexing. The man was fearless, and she decided it was the sexiest thing on earth.

Rebecca had always been afraid of everything, even social situations. Liam was the opposite, and she gravitated to his strength. He made her feel special, and her attraction to his rugged masculinity grew more by the second.

He whirled around once he stood up. "Are you okay, baby?" Liam held her shoulders, taking a good look at her even though the glow of the moon was faint. "I swear I can't catch a break when I'm with you."

She bit her lip before speaking. "What if he took you up on your offer? Would you let him take me?"

He cupped her face, his big, rough hands holding her securely. "I'll never let *anything* happen to you. If I had to, I'd kill them."

There was something in his eyes, in the way he said the words. He meant every word. Who was this guy?

"Maybe we should go," she said. With their luck, the jerks would come back with reinforcements. It was getting late, and a bit of chill was in the air. Liam said this was a popular spot, but in reality, it was in the middle of nowhere, pitch black, and she hadn't seen any teens.

"I want to be with you, Rebecca. Don't cut things short because of that. I have more to show you." He took her hand and led her farther down the rough path near the water. Crickets and frogs droned heavily from the underbrush. She closed her eyes briefly, the sound more soothing than any lullaby. Rebecca felt like a kid again, a young girl before the world brought her down. Back then she'd been happy in her skin, played in the dirt, and watched the stars past her bedtime. Then reality and adulthood stole all her magic. Something about Liam brought those feelings back.

He brought her into the heavier wooded area where the light of the moon didn't penetrate. She held his hand tighter, leaning into him so she didn't fall or bump into something. "How can you see?" she asked.

"These trails are imprinted in the back of my head. I've grown up in these forests."

She was new to the area, so she put her trust in him. After a bit more walking, he stopped dead. "Look."

Rebecca looked up when he tilted her chin up. There were fireflies everywhere, little lights scattered in the inky blackness, appearing and disappearing like magic. "They're beautiful," she said.

"The forest has a lot of secrets. I plan to show you every one of them." He played with her hair, his fingers brushing her cheek. Every time he touched her, she fell under his spell. She'd never given much thought to sex, not when she couldn't even talk with men. Now the wicked scenarios wouldn't leave her alone. His voice was so damn deep, the rough timbre making her clit tingle.

She touched his neck, her urge to be closer giving her the courage to do things she normally wouldn't dare to do. His skin was warm. "You feel good," she said. "Aren't you cold?"

"I'm fine. Are you?" He smoothed his hands down her arms, giving her goosebumps, but not from the cold.

"A bit." He interlocked their fingers with one hand. It felt like the most intimate thing in the world. Liam brought her hand up to his mouth and kissed it.

There were a lot of sounds around them in the bush—breathing, branches snapping. She hadn't paid much attention because she was falling in love with a stranger. But Liam suddenly stiffened, ushering her back the way they came. "We better get you home before you get a chill."

She frowned, wanting to stomp her feet like a two year old. In truth, she wanted the night to last forever, to feel his kisses again. "I thought the night was young."

"You were right. A gentleman shouldn't keep a woman out this late," he said. "We'll have to make a date for earlier next time."

At least there was a next time. She kept expecting him to realize he was out of her league, that she was too fat, or too awkward. But, no, he appeared genuinely interested.

He was quieter on the walk back, and she could feel the tension. When they reached the road after the short climb from the lake, he looked back into the darkness briefly.

"Are you okay?" she asked.

"I'm more than okay. I'm with the most beautiful woman in the world."

They drove back to her apartment. Her cheeks heated from the compliments. Even though she didn't believe everything he said, it still felt nice. She just hoped this fantasy wasn't like Cinderella because she never wanted it to end.

He came to a stop in front of her apartment.

"Thank you for taking me out. I loved it."

"Remember, I have a lot more to show you." He opened her door and helped her down. Liam hooked an arm around her, his hand at the small of her back. He held her close, their bodies practically pressed together. "And think about what I talked about. I want you, Rebecca. Want you as my woman."

Her mouth went dry. She didn't want to play hard to get. The voice in her head screamed at her to say "yes, yes, yes!" She would be a fool to reject this hunk of a man. But they'd only just met, and she didn't want him to think she was cheap if she moved too fast. She remembered the sharp talks from her mother about keeping her legs crossed and not looking men in the eye. She'd grown up with a complex around men and sex because of her overly strict, backwards upbringing.

"I'd like to get to know you better," she said.

He ran his tongue over his teeth. The dark shadow on his jaw and the wicked glint in his eyes held her spellbound. "That's exactly what I want, sweetheart. I want to know everything about you. When can I see you again?"

"I have a couple deadlines coming up this week, but I'll have more time on Thursday."

"Then I'll be here Thursday," he said. The man was a go-getter, and she had no intention to refuse him. She expected he got everything he wanted.

"Thanks again for taking care of me."

"That's my job." Under the glow of the moon, he leaned down and kissed her on the mouth. She supposed it was intended as a simple good-bye, but she wanted more. Rebecca wrapped her fingers around the collar of his shirt, pulling him down, deepening the kiss. His musky scent and scratchy stubble made her feel so feminine. He was a beast of a man, and she wondered if he was husky or muscular under the layers. She didn't care. Liam made her feel like a princess, and that wasn't an easy task. "You're already mine," he whispered against her lips. Then he stood straight.

"Maybe," she said. For the first time in a long time, life excited her. It wasn't shrouded in fears and uncertainties, just genuine joy.

"Get some sleep," he said. "And be careful when you leave the house. For a while, it would probably be best not to talk to strangers."

She found it an odd thing to say. Did he think she

was a crazy magnet, or was he already starting to be controlling? She'd rather stay single than deal with a fatal attraction. "I'll start going out in the afternoon instead of at night."

Rebecca had only gone shopping at night to avoid all the townsfolk, but Liam had given her enough confidence that she was going to give daytime shopping a go. She wanted to face her fears, not just look at life from behind a window.

"You have my number. Any time, day or night, call if you need me."

She nodded. He stayed on the sidewalk until she got inside the building. It was like going back in time when men were still gentlemen. Rebecca got to her third-floor apartment. Before she turned on her table lamp, she glanced down at the street. It was late, so the neighborhood was deserted. She hoped to see Liam drive away, but he was gone.

A wolf ran by in the distance. It was a massive black wolf cutting through the neighborhood. She let out a little gasp, hoping Liam didn't run into it. Being this far north, they weren't even safe outside the forests. She was definitely not heading out at night ever again.

She plopped down on her sofa and stared at the ceiling, lost in daydreams. Rebecca couldn't stop thinking about Thursday.

Chapter Four

Tracking through the woods over the next couple of days, Liam paid careful attention to any new scent. He hadn't liked how hunters or enemy packs had been lurking while he'd been on a date with Rebecca. The natural competition in wolves was often sparked to life before a male claimed his mate. They'd be able to sense his territorial threat, and their wolves would crave to compete for the prize. He'd never let anyone take Rebecca from him. There's no way his wolf would even allow it.

Just thinking about her was enough to make him so fucking hard. He wanted her in his bed as soon as possible. Over the past couple of days, he'd done nothing but think about her. How she'd feel beneath him. The scent of her skin. Her beautiful eyes. Her soft hair. He wondered about her pussy and how tight it would feel wrapped around his cock.

So far, she hadn't called him back about their second date. Thursday felt like a lifetime away.

He was obsessing. Combing through the surrounding forest and land, he had to make sure everything was safe for her. Two attacks within a short amount of time was just ridiculous. He'd never known that.

"What exactly are we looking for?" Jake asked

"If you remember, he said not to ask questions." Eli spoke up this time.

"Guys, shut up otherwise he's going to go all alpha on our asses," Ben said.

Liam had gotten his three best friends to help in the perimeter checks of their territory. Not only were they mated males but also good trackers. Shifters from other packs were getting too close to home. Too close to his mate.

"I've told you many times before you came out here. I need you to catch any scent at all and head in that direction."

"Trespassers would be crazy to enter your land," Ben said.

"There's a lot of crazy people around."

"You're not going to tell us what this is about?" Jake asked.

He remained silent, happy with his thoughts of Rebecca. He wasn't ready to share them with the pack just yet.

"Guys, haven't you smelled him?" Eli asked.

This made Liam pause and turn to look toward his group of friends. He didn't like this.

"He stinks like a woman. A human female."

Their gazes all landed on him, and he sighed. "So I met someone."

"A human someone," Jake said, inhaling the air. "She sweet? She smells sweet."

"It's been a couple of days. How the hell are you still smelling her?" With hands on his hips, he glared at the three mated males. If they'd not had females of their own, tonight could have ended differently.

"There are only two possible reasons," Jake said.

"Number one, she was wearing way too much perfume and it's kind of seeped into your pores and you need an extra shower," Eli said.

"Or two, she's your mate," Ben said.

"I'd go with two. He's been behaving like a mated male lately," Jake said.

"Which now makes us wonder, why you've been hiding her." Eli faced him. "We're part of your pack. We're not going to try and take her from you."

Staring at the three members of his pack that were

also his friends, Liam felt guilty. They'd each come to him when they found their woman that they loved, and yet he'd kept his a secret.

"Rebecca's not like any other woman. She's not pack. She's different."

"All of our women are different, Liam," Jake said.

"Rebecca struggles in social situations. She's not good around lots of other people. It's why I've not pushed the issue. Also, she hasn't called me again." He shrugged.

"You've been so damn busy with hunting things in the woods, would you have even answered?" Eli asked.

"Look, it doesn't matter. Until I know every single inch of this forest is safe, I'm not bringing her around. She seems to draw danger, and I'm not willing to risk her life for me." He saw his three friends wanted to argue, but he took off, tracing every step through the forest, trying not to think about how good she'd felt in his arms, or what he wanted to do to her when he finally got her alone.

For years, his pack had been left alone. Being a fierce alpha, not willing to be stepped on, he'd done right by his pack. They were loyal to him and him alone. He made sure they all had a good life without interference from the outside world.

Ben, Eli, and Jake had all become mated recently, and he was in the process of building their homes for them. Whatever they wanted, he'd make sure they got, and he was like this with all of his pack.

He may be alpha, but they were his family, and that meant he stuck by them.

His pack was worried about him. He smelled their concern but ignored it as he made his way out to the edge of the forest, taking a turn that allowed him to look down from the highest peak. Right there, above the tree line, he looked back, seeing his land and the town just past it. It was a thing of beauty to him. If he got the chance to have Rebecca here one day, she'd love it. He just knew she would. He wanted to open her world up to so much more.

She loved everything he'd shown her so far, and she'd not wanted their date to end. He'd been the one to bring it to a close for her own safety.

Glancing around the forest, he took a deep breath, and tried not to think about her. Rebecca was proving to be a distraction, albeit a good one.

"It's all clear," Jake said, startling him.

"When did you sneak up on me?"

"You think none of us remember what it was like to find our mate? How distracted we were? You're our alpha, and we won't let anything happen to you."

He stepped back through the thick set of the forest and stared at Jake.

"I won't let anything happen to the pack," Liam said.

"It's not wrong or weak to have someone watching your back. If for whatever reason our enemies are near, they'll use your distraction to their advantage. We can't allow that to happen."

"I won't ever allow any harm to come to any of you," Liam said.

Jake sighed. "Why is it so hard to accept help?"

"It's not hard."

"Then why won't you allow us to help you?"

He stared at his friend. He'd protected Jake a lot over the years. When they were little they'd been running out by the lake when a bear had stumbled onto them. Jake had a scar across his chest because the bear attacked before either of them could do anything. Liam recalled being scared. They'd only been nine at the time, but he'd attacked that bear and carried his friend back home where the pack nurse had healed him, and Jake made a full recovery. Just the sliver of an old scar remained on Jake now of that time.

It wasn't that he was afraid to take help.

To him, being the alpha, he was the one that protected, that made sure all of his pack were safe. They couldn't afford for him to be out of the loop.

"What do you suggest I do?" Liam asked.

"You know, pretending to take advice doesn't cut it."

"I've never had a mate before. I'm willing to take any advice that will help me with her. I don't know what to expect. How to deal with what I'm feeling. It's all new to me."

"Then in that case, you need to relax, and you also need to spend some time with her," Jake said.

"I will. When she calls."

"If she's your mate, your wolf won't allow prolonged distance."

This made Liam turn to Jake. He was the alpha, but being unmated, this was all new to him.

"How do you mean?"

"You said it's been a couple of days since you last saw her, right?"

"Yes."

"Your thoughts are about her? Have they diminished to nothing or are they getting stronger? Are you finding yourself thinking about her all the time? Those thoughts becoming more of a sexual nature? You want her more than anything else in the world?"

"What are you getting at?" Liam asked, feeling a little uncomfortable with how apt he was.

"Because if she's your mate and if your wolf

accepts that, it's only going to get worse. Distance doesn't help with a mated couple. You're going to have to spend time with her, a lot of time. I don't know if this is the same with human women. For us, me, Eli, and Ben, we've talked. We were all consumed with our need for our woman. It was like a fire burning beneath our skin, and we couldn't put it out. Only when we were around our woman would it help. If you don't visit this female soon, your wolf could snap, and make that decision for you. Last time I checked, one of us with our wolf in charge is not a pretty sight."

"I'd never hurt her."

"No, but seeing your wolf before she's ready, could damage her for life. You know this."

"She loves wolves."

Jake laughed. "When they're pretty, furry animals, not when they're trying to mate you." Jake slapped his shoulder. "Think about it."

****

Rebecca glanced at her cell phone and gritted her teeth. She'd been wanting to call Liam several times now, but each time she was worried that she'd sound more like a stalker. Were women supposed to make the first move after a date? How did she know the date went well? Did it go well? Toward the end of the night, he seemed to want to end it quite quickly.

Was that normal?

"Shut up!" She pressed her hands to her face. The computer screen glared at her with the next edit she must complete, and still, she was dragging her ass. She couldn't focus when all she could think about was Liam.

Tipping her head back, she took a deep breath, and tried to relax.

It was impossible to do.

How could she relax, not knowing what to

expect?

There was no way she'd be able to finish her work. Leaving her computer, she walked to the fridge and grabbed a bottle of water. Uncapping the lid, she took a long swig, all the time staring at her very silent phone.

Women weren't supposed to make the call, right? Would he just show up Thursday?

Rubbing her forehead, she tried to think of something else, of anyone else. Even the hero in the story she was currently editing had started to look like Liam. In fact, most of her thoughts were dominated by one man and one man alone.

"Stop being crazy." She walked back over to her computer, sat down, and stared, her fingers poised over the keyboard. She read the first line and nothing.

For thirty minutes she kept reading over that first line, and still she couldn't think of what to edit or write. None of the words were sinking in. This edit had been sitting in her inbox for three days. She normally had edits completed in no time, especially first round edits.

Picking up her cell phone, she ran her thumb across the screen, and brought up his number. Even as she shook her head, she pressed the call button, waiting.

If he didn't answer she'd either hang up or leave a message.

Starting to sound desperate.

Do you think other women call their dates?

What if he doesn't like me? Was he brushing me off by bringing me home early?

He felt that connection. I know he did.

"Hello," Liam said. His deep voice made her melt in her chair.

She'd never been connected to any man in her life, but just hearing him talk was enough to get her going. With being socially awkward, dating was out of the question. With no dating, sex was also out of the question. She could watch all the porn she liked, or dating shows, but not once had she gotten the chance to actually be with someone.

Liam, however, featured in a lot of her fantasies.

"Hey," she said. "It's me, Rebecca. You know, we went on a date the other night." *Please stop rambling, or you're going to make me sound like a loser.*

"How could I forget? I've been wanting to call you. I'm so sorry I've not been in touch."

"You did? Don't worry about it. I know we've got a lot on our plates. I've got this edit I really need to do." She was rambling again. *What a way to bore a guy.*

"I want to go out with you again," he said.

"You do?" *Don't act so surprised. You had an awesome time.*

"Do you want to go out with me again?"

His voice sounded so good. Delicious and deep. Her pussy grew slick just by listening to him, and not only that, she didn't want him to stop talking.

"Rebecca?"

"Yes, I'd love to go out with you."

"That's good, because I'm standing outside your door right now."

"Wait? What?" She looked behind her and stumbled across her living room, heading out into the corridor to check through the peephole. He was there. *Holy shit!* Liam stood outside her front door. He looked so sexy in the jeans and shirt he wore. The shirt was short sleeves, so she got a good look at his very muscular arms.

Her tits felt heavy, and the nipples tightened. She didn't know what was happening, but she opened the door, smiling at him. Turning off her phone, she didn't avert her gaze, not once. "You're here."

"I'm here. I was just passing through."

"You were?"

"No, I wasn't. I'm not very good with these things." He held up his cell phone. "They tend to piss me off, and when I want to see someone, I like looking them in the face. You're a very beautiful woman. I hope you don't mind."

"I tend to prefer these things, but for you, I'm more than happy to make an exception." She glanced down at her sweatpants and shirt. Her hair wasn't even brushed. She'd pulled it up on top of her head in a messy bun. "Shit, erm, I'm not dressed for you right now."

"You're going to send me away for you to look different?"

"I look like a slob."

"You look more than okay for me."

"Okay, no one can be that charming all in one." She rested her head against the door, watching him.

"Will you invite me in?"

"Are you a vampire?" She closed her eyes and shook her head. "You know what, scrap that. I don't seem to be thinking quite so clearly today. I'm putting it down to a lack of sugar."

"I'm not a vampire."

"Come on in then." She stepped behind the door and rubbed at her temple.

He's hot, and you're going to send him away with your weirdness. Get a grip, Rebecca.

Closing the door, she leaned against it.

Struggling around people made the most basic things seem like a challenge. Forcing a smile to her lips, she tried to figure out what to say next.

"Erm, coffee?"

"I'll take a tea, if you have any," he said.

"Yes, tea. Awesome. Okay, so I'll go and make it. Make yourself at home." She took a step away and grimaced. "Actually, don't make yourself at home."

"You are strange at this, aren't you?"

"Well, socially I've given you permission to do what you'd do at your own home. What I want you to do is sit and relax while I make us both a drink. I am completely ruining this moment right now, aren't I?" She pressed her lips together.

"Did you go to high school?" he asked.

"No. I was home-schooled. I've never been good with crowds. It's why I work from home, and you're the only person I've ever allowed here besides my parents. I try not to have them around all that often because they constantly tell me that I should be out and about, and they want grandkids."

"How about I come with you to the kitchen?"

"That would work."

She turned on her heel and left the room. Closing her eyes, she clenched her hands into fists, angry with herself. This was why she avoided everything to do with everyone. Her cheeks were on fire.

Filling up the kettle, she placed it on the stove. Turning toward him, she found him sitting on the kitchen counter, his hands together, thumbs twiddling around.

"If you want to leave, you can. I won't be offended." *I'll just cry because I'm not normal.*

"I'm here for you, baby. Why would I leave?"

"I'm just me, and no matter how much I wish I was different, I can't seem to stop this, and it sucks. It sucks to be me right now, and I hate that I feel this way." Her cheeks had to be bright red, and her eyes filled with tears. Everything felt a little too much right now.

With Liam at the coffee shop the other night and in the forest, she'd truly felt a connection. Like she was fighting whatever her problems were, but now, in her home, with him, everything was the same. She fucking hated it.

Suddenly, he stood in front of her. His hands cupped her face as he tilted her head back. She exhaled as he ran his thumb across her lips, and everything seemed completely frozen in time. She didn't want to move. Glancing from his eyes, which had taken on an amber glow, she looked at his lips. They were so firm.

More than anything she wanted those lips on her. To feel him kiss her, to take what he wanted. To make her forget how awkward she was acting.

Did he want her?

"I promised myself I'd give you time, that I'd let you get used to me."

"Time is overrated," she said. Placing her hands on his chest, she felt his rapidly beating heart. So powerful as it thumped beneath her fingers.

"I'm glad you said that."

Chapter Five

Liam couldn't keep away.

Jake had been right. The longer he spent apart from Rebecca, the more feral he became. His wolf was agitated beyond recognition, desperate for its mate. *Their* mate.

He kissed her in the middle of the kitchen, and she clung to him, his shirt bunched up in her little fists. The scent of her desire was potent, perfuming the air in a dizzying fog that had him nearly salivating for her pussy. Her sweet, virgin pussy.

"You smell sweet."

"It's my strawberry shampoo. I just took a shower."

He released the elastic from her hair and ran a hand through her long waves. It was only slightly damp. Her shampoo had nothing to do with her feminine signature, the scent calling out to his wolf.

Rebecca may be socially awkward, but once the heat turned up, her rigidity faded away, along with her nerves. Right now, she was putty in his hands, and after going days without seeing his woman, his body was pent up and hard for her.

Her tits pressed against his chest, soft and tempting. He'd been dreaming about stripping her naked and drowning in her softness. All he knew was she had to be marked by him. Until she was properly claimed, he'd obsess over another male stealing her away. His wolf demanded he fuck her and brand her with his bite.

"Forget the tea," he said. He leaned over and turned off the stove. "I'd much rather have you for a snack." Liam nipped her earlobe, before suckling it into his mouth. She moaned and tossed her head back.

"That feels good," she whispered.

"Then you're in for a surprise, beauty." He'd wanted to take her home and fuck her in his own bed now that his packmates had moved out of the house. But he had no doubt it would be happening here and now.

Liam teased her erogenous zones, determined to get her deeper into that sweet spot.

"I—I'm not good at this," she stammered. "I've never done any of this before."

"I'll teach you everything you need to know." He reached around and cupped her ass cheek. She had lush curves he could grab hold of. He squeezed the soft flesh. "Just relax for me."

It would be a challenge claiming a virgin when he wanted to fuck her hard and fast. He'd have to take his time, easing her into life as a mated woman. Liam wouldn't have it any other way, though. Knowing she was untouched by other males pleased him more than he imagined. His claim of ownership would be uncontested.

She held onto his biceps as he kissed along her jawline and neck, unable to get enough of her. When she started testing his muscles, he stepped back briefly and tugged off his t-shirt. "I'm all yours. Don't be shy." He took her hands and placed them on his chest, loving how her hands felt on his skin. She smoothed her fingers up over his shoulders, her eyes wandering all over his body. As she trailed her hands back down, she stopped at his belt and looked up at him.

"Your muscles are hard." She squeezed his arms again. "Strong."

"All the better to protect my woman." He tilted her chin up. "And you *are* my woman, Rebecca. You, this body, it's all mine."

She swallowed hard, but her desire didn't diminish.

"I'll never let anyone hurt you."

"I can't believe this is happening." Rebecca painted a fingertip down his chest as she bit her lower lip. Liam loved that she couldn't keep her hands to herself.

He grabbed her wrist. "I know you're new to this, but I don't think you understand the power you have over me. Every touch. Every move. You drive me crazy."

"I'm not trying to."

"You don't have to try. All I can think about is stripping you naked. Filling you with my cock." He reached between them and cupped her pussy through her pants. She gasped, bracing his shoulders.

"Liam…" She sank down onto his palm, her eyes rolling back in her head. "God, that feels good."

"We haven't even gotten started. Take your clothes off for me, Rebecca. I want to see you naked. All of you."

"You sure about that?"

"No teasing, baby. You've got me rock hard and painful."

She hesitated briefly, then pulled off her shirt and shimmied out of her jogging pants. "Is that good enough?"

He held her waist and took a good look at her. She wore a beige bra and panties, her red hair falling over one shoulder. Her tits spilled out the top and sides of her bra, and she clasped her hands in front of her stomach with a mix of shyness and need in her eyes.

"Not nearly good enough, little one. I want it all off. I want to see that pretty pussy and these gorgeous tits."

She cringed. "Just so you know, I wasn't exactly expecting this. Ever. I know most women shave down there, but I've never had a need."

He scowled, looking down at the front of her

panties and the dark shadow through the thin material. She was all natural, in every way. His wolf approved. "Even better." He motioned for her to keep going, to strip down to nothing.

She continued at a snail's pace, practically making him salivate. His muscles grew taut, his cock hard and throbbing. Rebecca unfastened her bra, those massive tits bouncing free, the nipples already tight bundles of nerves. Then she took a deep breath and wiggled out of her panties, leaving her perfectly nude.

"Holy shit, Rebecca. I never expected my mate to be this damn tempting."

"Really?"

"Come here." She stepped closer, and he pulled her against his body. Her soft tits, skin to skin against his chest, felt like heaven. He kissed her, holding her close. Liam slid his tongue in her mouth, deepening the kiss as he squeezed her ass with his free hand.

He reached down for her pussy, petting her curls before slipping one finger deep into her cunt. She tightened her hold on him, her mouth parting, and small, desperate pants escaping.

"You like that?"

She nodded, squeezing around his digit. His little minx wanted more, and he planned to give it to her. He added a second finger, slowly thrusting inside her tight little pussy. "That feels so good, Liam. So..." Her mewling was pure femininity.

He couldn't wait another minute to taste her. His fangs even pricked his gumline, his humanity threatening to fade away if he didn't satisfy his carnal needs. He slid his hands under her shoulders and hoisted her up onto the kitchen counter.

"Hook your feet on the edge," he said. Liam spread her thighs wide, all those curves begging for his attention. Her pussy glistened, pink and ripe. Holding her legs open, he knelt down and lapped up the folds.

"You don't want to do that."

He narrowed his eyes. "You have no idea how much I'm enjoying myself. I've been dreaming of you since our first date." Liam delved back in, holding her pussy lips apart so he could fuck her with his tongue. She squirmed and cried out as he suckled her clit. Liam was in fucking heaven, his head between his mate's thighs. He rubbed his face against her folds, wanting to drown in her scent. He ate her until she screamed loud enough to disturb the neighbors.

When she finally came, dishes fell to the ground as she flailed her arms to the sides, one mug shattering. "Liam!" Her screams were beautiful. He loved hearing her beg for him and wanted her to crave his cock as much as his tongue.

He continued to flick her clit until the waves of her contractions settled, and then he scooped her up into the cradle of his arms. "Where's the bedroom?"

She couldn't speak but pointed in the direction. He kicked open the door.

****

Liam dropped her down on her bed. It was only a double, so there wasn't much space. He stood at the end, looking down at her. There was something feral in his eyes, a look of hunger that made her pussy pulse again. She wasn't a lightweight, but he carried her as if she weighed nothing at all. His strength was a major turn-on.

He unbuckled his belt and unbuttoned his jeans. She stared, following that happy trail of hair from his navel down into his boxer briefs. After he kicked off his pants and boxers, his monster cock sprang free, hard as a branch. It bobbed slightly as he stepped closer. Her heart raced with anticipation, but there was no way she wanted this to stop.

Liam had shown her things she never expected to experience. He wasn't disgusted by her. In fact, she could feel his genuine attraction. The man made her feel like a queen. Rebecca hoped she didn't wake up to discover the past week had all been a dream.

"Show me my pussy," he said. His voice sounded deeper than usual, the timbre making her skin break out into gooseflesh. He made her feel dirty in a very good way. All her wicked fantasies were being realized.

She spread her thick thighs, holding her knees. The cool air hit her pussy, reminding her of how wet she was. Liam didn't come any closer. He ran his hands through his dark hair, all his muscles shifting deliciously as he moved. God, she wanted him. Wanted him deep inside her, making her his.

"Touch yourself."

"How?"

"Fuck yourself with a finger. Let me see, baby."

She bit her lip, her clit throbbing from his dirty talk. Rebecca obeyed, loving this game. She leaned up on her elbows, then carefully slid one finger inside her own cunt. In and out, she moved as instructed, watching his reactions. The man was stoic, his eyes dark and fixated.

"Like this?"

He nodded. "Just like that," he said. "Now taste yourself."

She couldn't help but gasp. Rebecca was tempted to refuse but was too invested in pleasing him. She brought her finger to her mouth and sucked it like a lollipop.

Did he just growl?

"Now lay back and cup those big tits of yours. Play with your nipples."

Rebecca dropped to her back and lifted her heavy

breasts up into her palms, using her thumbs to roll her nipples. Electric sensations skittered along her skin, traveling straight to her clit.

"Have you ever touched a man's cock before, Rebecca?"

"You're my first, Liam."

"And your last." He walked to the side of the bed, bracing one knee on the mattress. His cock was so close to her head she could see the bulging veins and drop of pre-cum at the tip. "Touch me. It's all yours."

She liked the sound of that. New, possessive feelings took her by surprise. She wanted Liam forever, only hers. Rebecca crawled up to her hands and knees, then sat on her heels in front of him. She petted his dick, the silky soft skin not what she expected. She attempted to wrap her fingers around his girth, but he was too big and hard.

He fascinated her. She pumped his cock in slow movements, watching his foreskin expose the mushroom head. He reacted now, groaning with each stroke of her fist. She loved how this beast of a man responded to her touch. It empowered her. "Does it feel good, Liam?"

"More than you could ever know."

After she pumped him a few more times, he stilled her hand. "Taste me, baby. I want to see your lips around my cock."

She leaned forward on her knees and licked the tip. His dick jumped. This was new to her, and she didn't want to screw up or look like an amateur. She didn't want him comparing her to other women he'd had. Rebecca wrapped her lips around the head of his cock and sucked, taking as much of him down her throat as she could without choking. He combed his fingers into her hair, groaning and growling as he directed her movements. He tasted earthy and all male.

"That's enough," he said with clenched teeth. "I need to be inside you."

"Okay." Her nerves ramped up. Liam was massively hung, and she'd never had a man. But this was going to happen, and if what she'd experienced so far was any indication, she'd love every minute of sex with him.

He hoisted her up higher in the bed and crawled over her, his body lean and muscled to perfection. The faint scent of his cologne was the ultimate aphrodisiac. She breathed him in, kissing his neck when he lowered over her. His erection pressed against her inner thigh as he took residence between her legs.

"I love your body." He lifted one breast up and sucked her nipple and areola into his hot mouth. Liam teased her with his wicked tongue until she arched her back and combed both hands into his hair. He trailed kisses up her chest to her neck, then suckled her erogenous zone. "Tell me you're ready to be claimed." He whispered in her ear between kisses.

"I'm ready." He leaned back a bit, and they looked into each other's eyes. "Just for you, Liam. I'm not the kind of girl to jump into bed with a man, even if we've moved really fast. I want you to know that."

He smiled. "Fate does that to a person. Your body knows what it wants."

Liam positioned his cock at her entrance, their eyes still locked. He pushed in, her moist pussy helping him ease inside. She immediately felt the fullness, but she tried not to flinch.

"You're big," she said, smoothing her hands over his back.

"Am I hurting you?"

"I'm okay." Damn, she'd never been this full, every cell touched by his cock. When he was fully seated, all those thick inches deep inside her, he paused.

"You're so tight around my dick, baby. You feel like heaven."

Rebecca had the sudden realization that she was no longer a virgin. It took her long enough at thirty years old, but honestly, she'd expected to die untouched. She'd moved out to the boondocks to get away from the hustle and bustle, but she never expected to find a man to love and protect her.

She could feel his erection throbbing inside her, and she could only imagine the amount of restraint a virile man like Liam was using. She wiggled a bit, pulling his neck down to kiss him. "Fuck me," she said against his lips.

His chest rumbled, then he pulled out a few inches and sank back in. Over and over, he pistoned in and out in a slow, deliberate rhythm. It didn't take long for her nerves to disappear, replaced by a heady lust. She needed him, wanted to be owned by him. Rebecca had no one else in the world. She rarely saw her parents, and they only reminded her of the strict, rigid upbringing. They never nurtured her insecurities, but made her feel like an outcast, forcing her to act "normal". Liam understood her, didn't push her away because she was different. He was like a breath of fresh air in her life.

"I'm different, Rebecca. Different from other men. But I'll never hurt you."

She liked him exactly as he was. "It's okay, Liam. Kiss me again." They kissed hard and demanding. His powerful arms supported his weight over her, the thrusting of his hips picking up. She spurred him on, digging her heels into his hard ass.

"You want more, baby?"

"I think I *need* more."

Liam delivered, fucking her like a stud horse. Her

old bedframe creaked and groaned as he pounded into her pussy. Each time he came down, his pubic bone rubbed her sensitive clit. An explosion of sensation pulled her from reality. "Let me mark you. Tell me to mark you."

She wasn't sure what he was talking about, but she trusted him and wasn't ready to refuse anything at this point. "Do it," she commanded.

He licked the base of her neck, and then a sharp pain stole her erotic fog for a moment. She struggled, but he held her wrists at the side of her head, his cock deep inside her pussy.

"Ouch!"

He'd bitten her. She hadn't expected that from him. Within seconds the pain morphed into a rush of heat so powerful that a second orgasm barreled to the surface. She screamed, the contractions rushing through her body like the waves of a tsunami. Her pussy squeezed around Liam's cock, milking him as he joined her in orgasm.

When the lust settled, her breathing was labored, her entire body covered in a sheen of clean sweat. "You bit me," she said between pants. He rolled to the side, his sticky release on her thigh.

"Marked you," he corrected. Liam lay on his side beside her. He touched the wound on her neck. "We're bonded for life, Rebecca. This mark is my promise to you."

That sounded better. His sweet words soothed her insecurities, making her feel right with the world. He was unorthodox, but with skills like his, she wasn't going to complain.

"People change," she said. "No one tends to stay in my life very long."

"Not me." He brushed the moist hairs from her face. "There will never be another woman for me."

She cuddled into the crook of his arm, excited about the future.

Chapter Six

The scent of her intoxicated him. Liam had been warned by his friends to be careful. No one knew how a human female would handle such a mating, but the bite he gave her was almost healed and his cock thickened just remembering the feel of her pussy wrapped around his dick. He'd been her first.

The way her tight cunt had given way to him would stay with him forever. She belonged to him now, and he'd never let her go, not ever.

Running his fingers across the mark that claimed her as his, he smiled. It looked so beautiful, so right, so perfect.

He'd been dreaming about doing it for some time, and now that he actually had, it gave him a whole new thrill. This was his mate. The one chosen to love him, and he fucking relished it. She was perfect in every single way.

She released a little moan, and he watched as she woke up. He smiled down at her.

"Hey," she said. "You're awake."

"Watching you sleep."

"That's not creepy at all."

He shook his head. "Not at all."

She lifted her arms up above her head, giving a little stretch and yawning at the same time. He stared down at her naked, full tits. Running his hand up her chest, he cupped one and teased the nipple, savoring her moan.

"That feels so good."

"You feel good, baby. So fucking good. I love your tits."

"You do?"

He leaned down and licked one perfectly beaded

nipple, smiling as she gasped. Her fingers sank into his hair. "I don't say stuff I don't mean. They're perfect. So perfect." He pinched the tip before licking away the pain with his tongue.

She arched up, thrusting her tit into his mouth, and he couldn't get enough.

His cock hardened within seconds, the tip already leaking pre-cum. He wanted inside her again, filling her pussy with his cum, getting her pregnant. She'd look so hot with his child inside her, swollen, ready to give birth. The need to impregnate her was so damn strong. He couldn't fight it, nor did he want to.

"Please, Liam, I need you. I need you now."

Sliding his hand down her body, he found her wet pussy. Teasing her clit, he stroked back and forth getting her more aroused by the second. Moving down, he filled her pussy, plunging a finger within her, feeling her tight walls wrapping around him.

Adding a second finger, stretching her open, he watched her ride up as she moaned his name repeatedly.

"I want you to come all over my fingers first, baby." She needed to be really wet. She was still so new at this, and he didn't want to hurt her. Her pussy had taken him once, but a second time would hurt her unless she was really wet. She'd be sore and his scent would be all over her. Any passing wolves would know she belonged to him and should keep them away. There could be a few that would try to rival the claim, especially as his mating with her was so new.

You're going to have to tell her the truth.

He didn't know if he could do that.

Even though she loved wolves, it would still be a challenge to do this. She was human. Wolves were something from fairy tales. They were not to be taken seriously. Not to humans.

She cupped his face. "What's wrong?"

"Nothing's wrong."

"You started to frown. I think you even growled."

"Sorry. I didn't mean to scare you."

"You don't scare me, Liam. Far from it." She pressed a kiss to his lips. "I find everything you do really sexy."

"You do, do you?"

She nodded, biting her lip. "Yes."

"You like it when I do this."

He pressed his lips against her neck, giving her a bit of a bite. She moaned, tilting her head to the side, giving him better access.

"Yes, that feels so good. Don't stop."

"What feels good?" he asked. "This?" He rubbed his thumb against her clit. "Or this?" He sucked on her neck right over her pulse.

She cried out. "Both. I love them both."

"Then tell me to fuck your pussy and kiss you."

"Fuck my pussy and kiss me."

"Please."

"Please, Liam, please."

He slammed his lips down on hers, stroking her clit as he did. Breaking from the kiss, he sucked on her neck, moving between her thighs as he trailed his lips down her body, licking her body between kisses.

She wriggled about, and he loved it. He loved watching her squirm, but also tasting her. Pulling his fingers from her pussy, he licked them, savoring her.

"So fucking good. I need more."

Spreading her legs open wide, he used his shoulders to keep her open as he ate her pussy. She was already getting wet, but he wanted her so slick that it was dripping onto the bed. His cock was painfully hard and he wanted to be so deep inside her, but first, he wanted her to come, to scream his name, to have it echoing around the walls so he couldn't think of anything else.

Gliding his tongue down, he thrust inside her, relishing her cries of pleasure as he ravished her pussy.

"I'm so close."

"Then come for me, baby. I want to hear you scream it. Give it to me." He attacked her clit, glancing up her body as she moaned and whimpered. He wanted her so badly as she wriggled on his mouth.

When she came, it was a beautiful sight to behold, one he couldn't help but love as his name filled the air at the same time as her cream flooded his mouth. He drank her up, pushing her into a second orgasm.

Only when she was over the crest of her second did he grab his cock and crawl between her thighs. Running the tip up and down her pussy, he stared into her eyes as he filled her once again.

Her tight little cunt squeezed him like a vise. He slammed to the hilt inside her only to pull out and slide back in, going deeper than before.

She wrapped her legs around his waist, and he rocked inside her, staring into her eyes. He kept checking to make sure she wasn't hurting. He didn't want to harm his mate. He wanted her completely blown away by the pleasure he was giving her.

"Please, it feels so good. God, so good." She thrust up to meet him, and he caught her hands, holding them against the bed as he took over.

Seeing her need for him, he gave her everything, not holding back, pushing in deep.

"Yes, yes, please, I need you. Please, Liam."

He didn't know if this was part of the mating, but it was like she was calling to his wolf. Begging him to come inside her, needing that claiming that only he should understand. Her grip on his hands tightened. She arched up, wanting him, begging for more.

Driving inside her over and over again, he watched as she built to another orgasm. He changed the angle so he rubbed against her clit as he thrust in deep.

It wasn't enough.

He needed to be closer to her.

Releasing her hands, he wrapped his arms around her so that they were body to body. He'd never felt anything this strong before, nor this fast. It should terrify him, but it didn't. In fact, it made him so fucking happy.

He'd finally found her. The one that was his woman.

"Please, Liam," she said.

"You want my cum, baby? You want me to fill your pussy?"

"Yes."

He claimed her lips as he fucked her hard, going as deep as she could take him. Her nails scored his back, and his wolf within him howled in pleasure. They wanted her marks, to wear them like a fucking badge of pride. She belonged to him, and they were going to treat her with so much love. She'd never want for anything.

He'd make sure of it.

This was why his friends were the way they were. They had something to fight for. She was fucking everything to him and more.

They would be bound together for all eternity.

Liam thrust inside her one final time, feeling his seed pulse as it filled her body.

I want a baby.

I want a wife.

I want everything.

He wanted it all with this woman in his arms. He'd never had anything precious to him before, but now he did, and he didn't want to lose that. He loved her more than anything.

Pushing some of her hair off her face, he smiled down at her.

"Hey, beautiful," he said.

"That was amazing. I don't know what came over me. I just felt something overwhelming, and I needed you."

"How do you feel now?"

"So much better." She cupped his cheek. "I love being with you. It's like everything else falls away and I don't have to worry anymore."

"You'll never have to worry again." He stroked her cheek. "You can always rely on me, Rebecca. Always."

"I'm not like other women. I'm not normal."

"Normal is overrated, and I'm not here for other women, Rebecca. I'm here for you."

****

This was a big mistake. Rebecca tried to think of something, any excuse that would stop the car, and make him turn around so that she could go back home. Home to her perfectly ordered world that didn't have any other family. Where for a few short minutes she could pretend to be like other people and not have any issue.

"What's wrong?" he asked.

"Nothing."

"You're fidgeting like mad, and I know you're lying."

"How do you know that?"

"I just know."

She'd noticed he seemed to have a sense of something, whenever she was upset or annoyed, or even worried. In the past couple of days, she'd gotten used to him being around the house. He'd stayed, and they'd made love, had sex, and ordered takeout food because neither of them wanted to be away from the other long enough to cook.

These feelings she had for him were entirely foreign to her. She didn't even know if they were normal, if this feeling of needing to be with him all the time was natural. Not only that, each time they had sex, she had this overwhelming desire for him to come within her. To mark her. Clearly, all the years of editing books were starting to get to her.

She knew it would happen.

The lonely nights.

All the secret fantasies she had.

It all would lead to a moment when she finally had a boyfriend that she'd just explode with need.

Well, it had happened, and now she was so embarrassed. Even though she didn't want to go and meet his family, her body needed him. Holding his hand didn't exactly help matters as she knew just how good it felt for him to touch her, to stroke her, to be inside her. They were both insatiable, and one glance at his cock, and she saw that he was having the same kind of trouble. His cock pressed against the front of his jeans, and she wanted him inside her once again.

"Don't you think it's a bit early to, you know, meet your friends?"

"I wanted you to also see my place. My friends will be there as well. We can ignore them though."

She tucked some hair behind her ear, not really liking that idea. Not liking it at all. She was so nervous. What if they didn't like her? What if they hated her? She didn't want Liam to choose between her or his friends. That would be wrong.

Why are you panicking?

Stop being weird right now.

They'd already started down the long trek of

forest. She'd heard a lot of rumors about these places and wolves attacking hikers. She was of the mind that the forest was a wolf's habitat and anyone who invaded it kind of got what was coming to them. If someone invaded her home, she'd be so pissed. She also had a large baseball bat in case something like that ever happened. Of course, it hadn't yet, but she liked to be prepared for everything that might happen.

He drove for another ten minutes, and when he pulled up in front of a large A-frame log cabin, she was in shock. She didn't know what she expected, but it certainly wasn't the luxury house before her.

"You live here?"

"Yes, all my life now."

"Wow, it's beautiful."

"You've not seen inside yet. Hopefully it's not a mess." He pulled the jeep to a stop and turned off the ignition.

She waited as he climbed out of the truck, walking around to her side, and helping her out. Within seconds, Alphie was there, and she smiled, bending down to give the large dog a stroke.

"You're such a cute boy."

"He's missed me. This is the longest I've ever been away," said Liam.

"Now I just feel bad."

He wrapped an arm around her waist, kissing her neck.

Don't think naughty things.

Think about dogs and puppies.

Not what it feels like to have this man between my thighs.

Just one thought of thighs and she whimpered, envisioning his beautiful cock sliding in deep.

He released a growl, and that only aroused her

more. She noticed he growled a lot. Rather than it scaring her, she found it highly arousing and masculine.

"So, you finally decided to come back."

She pulled away from his kiss at the sound of another man.

Glancing toward the house, she saw three men standing on the wraparound porch.

"Where are your women?" Liam asked.

"Out for the day. They had to get some shopping done," another said. "Is this her?"

Another on the left sniffed the air. "Holy shit, you don't waste any time, do you?"

She found that weird. What was with all the air sniffing?

"Rebecca, I'd like you to meet my very weird friends that have, for some reason, seemed to have forgotten they're dealing with a *human*. That's Jake, Ben, and Eli."

Jake had been the sniffer.

Eli the questioner.

Ben had yet to speak.

Holding her hand up in a wave, she smiled at them. "Hey."

They all stood watching her.

"Did I do something wrong?" she asked.

"No, they have no manners." Liam took her hand. "Come on, let me show you the house while they remember what to do when they meet someone for the first time."

She found it odd the way they bowed their heads as she passed or that they wouldn't look at her.

Was she too ugly for them?

None of this made any sense.

She was soon distracted though as they entered his home. It was beautiful, breathtaking in fact. Glancing around the open home, she couldn't help but smile. The kitchen was huge and opened up onto a large, open concept dining room. The ceilings peaked high above them, and a stone fireplace traveled all the way up. Oversized glass windows offered a picturesque view of a valley and river below.

"Do you have a lot of guests?" she asked.

"Yes. I come from a large family. The guys outside are friends and family."

"I don't think they liked me."

Liam pulled her into his arms. "They adore you. They just don't know how to act yet. They will. I promise." He leaned down, kissing her lips.

He took her on the tour of the ground floor, showing her the sitting room, library, and his office. There was also a games room with a pool table. It was like he didn't have to leave the house as he had everything at his fingertips.

To Rebecca, this was sheer heaven.

She loved it, right down to how secluded it was from the world. When he took her upstairs, the bedrooms were also beautiful.

"They kept it clean then."

She giggled at his sigh. "You were worried?"

"They were all staying with me, along with their women. It has seemed a little full at times."

This made her laugh.

"What do you think of the place?"

"What do I think? It's perfect. I don't even know how anyone could hate it, or even be upset by it. I think it's amazing. So beautiful. I bet you get a lot of peace out here, don't you?"

"I do. It's nice. We also get a lot of travelers and hunters that can be a pain."

"Is that because of the wolves?"

"What do you know about the wolves?" he asked.

"Not a lot. I know they've been known to attack tourists and travelers."

"You still like them?"

"Of course. I haven't really met one before though," she teased. "I don't imagine I ever will. You know, the whole snarling and wanting to kill being a bit of a turn off."

"I bet there are a lot of wolves that would love you," he said, pulling her close. They were on the upper landing leading to the wooden stairs.

She smiled. "You know how to say all the right words, Liam." She pressed her hands to his chest and went on her tiptoes to kiss him. "And I for one love that."

Someone cleared their throat.

"It would seem my friends have decided to be normal and now want to introduce themselves."

She giggled again. Whenever she was around him she felt so relaxed to be herself. "We could ignore them if you'd like. I don't mind doing what you want to do," she said.

The bedroom was calling her. *His* bedroom.

He groaned. "That's really tempting."

She ran her hand down his chest, loving his moan as she cupped his dick.

"You do know we can hear you, right?" one of them said.

Liam sighed. "Their timing is the worst thing in the world."

"That it is." She withdrew her hand. "I guess we should go and see them."

He gripped her ass and claimed her lips once again. Wrapping her arms around his neck, she felt alive in his touch. Like he'd finally awakened a part of her that had been dormant all of her life. This was supposed to be. The two of them together.

She felt possessive, desperate, and needy. So fucking needy.

Chapter Seven

He wanted to fuck Rebecca again, to christen his bedroom, but he could wait. He'd gone a lifetime without a woman of his own, so a few more hours wouldn't kill him.

"Let me show you around the property," he said. They held hands as he took her out the back door. She'd done well with his friends. He'd worried about her feeling anxious and wanting to leave. It pleased him how she handled herself, and that she loved his home. It would soon be *their* home.

"It's like a dream here," she said. "Heaven."

Liam had the perfect spot for the homestead. His packmates' new cabins were out of sight, but not too far off. There was plenty of space for privacy. He'd had enough of stepping on toes for the past year with six extra people in his house. No way could he stomach listening to them fuck another day. Going forward, the main house was for his *own* family.

Pinecones and leaves littered the forest floor, but it would soon decompose into new black earth. He remembered his father telling him the legend of the great oak, showing him a small acorn and explaining how it would one day grown mighty. His father had done a lot to prepare him to become alpha, to take his rightful place in the pack. Liam knew full well the importance of keeping the bloodline alive. It was one of many reasons he was thankful for finally finding Rebecca. One thing he'd never been taught was how to prepare for a human mate.

"Most women think it's too rural here, too far from shopping malls and nail salons," said Liam.

She shook her head. "That's not me. I left the city because it was too much to handle. The noise, the pollution, the fake smiles. I couldn't do it anymore." Rebecca bent down by the river, running her fingers through the crystal-clear water. "This is real. I don't have to pretend to be someone else."

He tilted his head. "Who would you be?"

"I don't know. The woman on magazine covers—beautiful, confident, and refined."

"You're all that and more." He sat down on the riverbank, wrapping his arms loosely around his knees.

"Do you know me at all?"

He smiled. "Baby, I don't want a fake woman. You're natural, honest, and perfect exactly the way you are. Don't change."

She flicked some water at him and giggled. The sound made his cock hard. Breeding her kept creeping into his thoughts, and he hoped he'd already impregnated his mate.

"It's so quiet here. All I can hear are birds and insects." She closed her eyes and breathed in deeply. "Do you ever get scared living this far off the grid?"

"Never."

She turned and smirked at him. "You're fearless, aren't you?"

"I'm only afraid of losing you."

Her smiled faded as she stared back at him. "I'm surprised you're still single. You said you're around my age?"

"Maybe a bit older. Does it matter?" Liam had recently turned fifty. Although shifters didn't age as quickly as humans, the number still sent him into a tailspin. His biological clock was ticking, and he'd been the only one in his pack left unmated—until now.

"No, it doesn't matter at all. I'm just curious."

"What if I told you I'm fifty? Twenty years older than you."

She bit her lip. "I'd say you've taken very good care of that body." Rebecca winked at him before returning to the water. He couldn't believe the weight that lifted from his shoulders. He swore she'd be turned off by his true age.

"The forest looks good on you," he said.

"I'm kind of surprised how much I love it out here. I've never been camping, never roasted marshmallows, or ate over an open fire. My anxiety kept me from doing a lot of things in my life."

"Things are going to change now. I'll make sure of it," he said.

Rebecca stood and came over to him. She knelt down and straddled his lap, wrapping her arms around his neck and kissing him hard, her tongue pushing in his mouth. "Teach me everything."

He was about to roll her to her back when his peripheral vision picked up movement. Two wolves dashed through the underbrush toward his home, barely disturbing a leaf. A human would never have been able to notice them—Liam was not human. He held Rebecca a little tighter as his wolf thrashed within him. There were trespassers on his land, and that was one thing he would not tolerate, especially now that he was a mated male.

Liam got to his feet, pulling her up with him. She looked disappointed. "We should get back to the house," he said.

"Already?"

"We'll have lots of time to explore. Promise. I just need to check up on something quickly." His senses were working on overdrive. He wanted to shift, to chase after the threats and eliminate them. It felt like a thousand miles to the house when they were only a few minutes away.

Once they got to the back door, he brought her to the kitchen and opened the fridge. "Help yourself, baby. There's plenty to eat. I promise I won't be long. Be back before you know it." He kissed her forehead.

He walked away from the house into the tree line before shifting into his alpha wolf. Power surged through his veins as his beast took control. His muscles stretched, his bones reforming as he changed from man to wolf. All his senses became magnified as he tracked the trespassers. The other packs knew damn well where the property lines started and ended. Why were they pushing their luck? Liam had a reputation for a reason.

Jake appeared, followed by Eli and Ben. His men were trained and lethal. They may be like docile pups with their women, but they were dangerous when it came to protecting their territory. The Grey Valley Pack was known as one of the deadliest wolf packs, and they were rarely challenged.

"They're heading south," said Jake. *"We'll be able to catch up before they hit the mountains."*

"Let's fuck them up," said Eli, his wolf pawing the ground in anticipation.

"We all have mates now. Trespassers will not be tolerated, especially shifters." Liam led the charge, all four of them racing after the two wolves.

He couldn't wait to get back to Rebecca, to learn everything about her. They had the rest of their lives to discover each other, and he looked forward to the years to come. He wondered if any of their children would have her red hair. Would they even be shifters? Liam didn't know of any other human-shifter matings, so this was all new to him.

He had to keep focused on his task. It was time to lay down the law, to make other wolf packs aware that any trespassing would not be tolerated. He couldn't turn a blind eye now that he had a woman to think about. She always had to come first.

"These fuckers don't give up," said Ben. They'd been running for about half an hour, following the distinct trail. Every so often he'd catch a glimpse of the wolves through the trees.

They slowed down when a parked vehicle came into view in the near distance. The only trail out this far was an old, abandoned mining road leading to the mountains.

Two humans sat in the truck, the engine revving to life.

"The trail stops here," said Liam. He didn't have a good feeling about this.

The passenger lowered his window halfway, laughing mockingly. "Our alpha was right. You'd chase us to hell and back, wouldn't you? But I count four wolves, so how many are watching your female?"

Liam leapt up against the window, managing to claw the man's face before the truck barreled forward, leaving a wake of dust and debris.

He shifted into his skin, pacing, running his hands through his hair. His heart raced, and it felt like a vise squeezed his chest to the point he could barely breathe. "They planned this," he whispered more to himself than his men. "They led us out here on purpose. The chase, the waiting vehicle, Rebecca alone at the house."

"You couldn't have known. They must have planned this for a while," said Jake.

"Fuck! Even running full speed, it'll take half an hour to get home. They must have her by now." He'd failed. Failed as a mate, an alpha, a man. If his rivals thought he was pissed off before, he'd be bringing hellfire to their world if anything happened to Rebecca.

"Time's wasting," said Eli. "Let's hope it's not

too late."

****

Her pussy ached. She needed Liam, but he took off right when they'd been making a connection. She hoped everything was okay.

There was a lot of meat in the fridge. It looked like the man was a carnivore. She found some fruit in a cooler drawer, so grabbed a green apple. Rebecca acquainted herself with the luxury kitchen, finding a knife in a nearby drawer. She washed the apple, then cut it on the granite counter while enjoying the view out the back windows. Maybe they could cook something together later rather than getting takeout. In a kitchen like this, it would be a pleasure to make a meal. Her apartment had a tiny nook for a kitchen.

She took a bite of the fruit as she wandered around the great room. Even though it was big and luxurious, it had a cozy, rustic feel. There was a lot of wood, rich colors, and natural finishes. It was her first time in the cabin, and she already felt more at home than she had in places she'd lived in for years.

As she savored the views, she saw Alphie come up from the river. He was limping, struggling to get up the slope. Rebecca put her food down on the coffee table and rushed out the back door and down the slope toward the dog.

"Alphie!"

The dog kept limping towards her, but once she was out in the open, far away from the house, she realized she wasn't alone. She swallowed hard as she took in her surroundings. There were three men closing in on her. Alphie tried to protect her, growling despite his injury, but he was in no shape to take on these men. The one to her right smirked, and a shiver crept up her spine. She knew these were no friends of Liam's.

"This is the one all right," said the man. He took a deep breath. "No mistaking it."

"He could be heading back by now," said the tallest man.

The first guy shook his head. "Rolly and Hector are taking them on a good ol' goose chase. Liam's getting sloppy in his old age. He left his mate unsupervised."

"Better for us," said the man to her left. She turned to look at him, seeing a twisted grin on his face. She felt dirty just looking at him, and Rebecca wanted no part of any of these men.

"What do you want?" she asked.

"Leverage. We'll have Liam eating out of the palm of our hands once he finds out you're missing."

She scowled, feeling more pissed off than scared. "And I suppose you assholes are the ones to hurt his dog."

"It's just a fucking dog."

Rebecca crossed her arms over his chest. "Stay away from me." She attempted to reverse course back to the house, but they made a circle around her and started closing in. She kept looking off into the distance, wondering how long until Liam got back home. He'd said he wouldn't be long.

Why did she have the worst luck in the world? In the past week she'd been threatened three separate times. Liam had saved her the first two times, but she had a sinking feeling she was fresh out of luck.

"Nobody has to get hurt. Behave and we won't have a problem."

Rebecca narrowed her eyes at him. She was no match for three men, but she wasn't just going to leave with them willingly. Everyone knew the worst thing to do was let an attacker take you to a second location. She had no idea what their intentions were, and she didn't want to find out.

After walking backwards for as long as she could, she turned and bolted, running toward the house. She'd never been athletic, so she didn't get far. One of the men pounced on her, knocking her to the ground. Her breath rushed from her lungs, leaving her gasping, but she kept crawling forward. A hand around her ankle kept her from getting to her feet. She kicked back with her other leg, making contact. The man screeched, and then they were all on her, securing her against her will. A black sack was forced over her head, blocking off her sight. Her arms and legs were pinned as she was hauled off into the forest. They dropped her over a man's lap, and an engine starting up under her made her yelp.

The terrain was rough, the ATV jostling and jolting through the overgrown forest paths. She'd finally found happiness with Liam, and now everything was falling apart. Rebecca just wanted to be happy. Now she wasn't sure she'd even survive the night.

Why did they hate Liam so much? Why did her boyfriend have so many damn enemies? She hardly knew him, but at this point, she'd love him even if he turned out to be a criminal. He'd never made her feel scared or unwanted. Liam had single-handedly introduced her to life without fear, and she was finally coming to peace with herself.

She lost track of time as they drove through the forest. She considered flinging herself off the ATV, but with her luck, she'd probably get run over or worse. When they slowed to a stop, she was forced over the guy's shoulder, and he dumped her into the back of another vehicle. The air in her sack was getting stale.

"Drive," he said.

Oh God, where are they taking me?

So many memories flashed in her head during the drive. She'd come so far in the past five months living here, and even more in the past week. No more medication, and her virginity was history. Liam showed her pleasures she never knew existed.

She lifted up the corner of her sack for air and to see her surroundings. Luckily, the man sitting next to her was looking out his window. She scanned the area. They were on a main road now. She recognized some of the landmarks. It's not like she had a cell phone or anyone to give her location to. What she needed was opportunity. As soon as she had a chance, she'd make a break for it. The thought of rape, torture, and murder was worth fighting to avoid at all costs. Normally a situation like this would have put her into a full-blown panic attack, but ever since Liam committed to her, she felt as if she could take on the world.

And she still had hope her Prince Charming would save the day again. She'd always been a hopeless romantic, but she'd reserved those feeling for romance novels, not real life. Liam changed everything.

"We're here," said her captor. She wondered where the other two men had gone. Her odds were better with one.

He dragged her roughly out of the pickup truck and tugged off the sack. Her eyes adjusted to the daylight, and her lungs filled with fresh air. They were in the forest again, a wooden hut just ahead. Several wolves crept in from between the trees. She turned to the man squeezing her arm, but he only laughed at her.

Were they going to feed her to the wolves? What would that prove?

She struggled, twisting and squirming to get out of his firm grasp. "Let me go!"

"She doesn't know," said the driver of the truck.

Neither man showed any fear of the wild animals moving in. Were they trained?

"Even more fun." He squeezed her arm tighter, giving her a sharp shake until she settled down. She remembered Liam telling her some wolves would love her. These looked at her like she was on the menu.

"You guys are in big trouble. Let me go and I won't say anything." She tried to sound tough, but it came out all wrong.

"Did Liam tell you what marking you signified?"

She frowned. "Of course. He loves me. I'm his … mate." It sounded dumb coming from her, but from Liam it sounded sexy as hell.

"Only werewolves mark their woman with a love bite. Haven't you read a single fucking fairy tale? I thought human girls ate that shit up."

"This is real life."

One of the wolves stood on two legs, shaking and morphing before her eyes. Its hair receded and bones elongated. Within seconds the wolf had turned into one of the men by the river. Her mouth fell open, and her entire body went numb. Thoughts and memories overloaded her mind as she tried to make sense of what she'd witnessed. Everything she'd ever known or understood was in question, and it was too much to process.

"You've been kept in the dark," he said. "You'd think when a werewolf claimed a mate he'd have the decency to fill her in on the facts." He tutted.

Her captor said, "If all goes well, he'll come for you. That's what we're counting on. Hope you enjoyed the honeymoon while it lasted because Liam's about to go to doggy heaven."

She shook her head, dizziness washing over her in waves. "No, Liam's not a wolf."

They all laughed and mocked her. "He's a legend around here. Honey, your man is an *alpha* wolf."

Chapter Eight

"You go and it'll be a trap," Jake said.

"I can't just sit here. They've got my mate, Jake." He gripped the back of the chair and threw it across the room.

Alphie was hurt and nursing his injuries. They'd hurt his fucking dog and taken his woman. Liam was so fucking pissed right now. The need to hurt, to kill was so fucking strong. Rebecca's scent was all over the house, but with her gone, it was slowly fading. He had to find her. To get her back.

There's no way he could let anything happen to her. His father's wisdom filtered through the anger. He'd told Liam that a man could tell when he was in love when protecting someone else was more important than protecting himself. He felt that for Rebecca.

"You know this poses a lot more problems," Eli said.

"I know." Liam didn't need to be told what he faced.

"She'll know the truth now," Ben said.

He closed his eyes, counted to ten, then looked at Ben. "I know."

Ben held his hands up. "I wasn't trying to state the obvious or anything."

"Then what the fuck were you trying to achieve? She's in the hands of my enemy, and you fuckers don't seem to get that I'm having a really hard time right now. I'm trying to deal with the fact she's gone."

He turned his back on them, feeling the primal need to release his wolf.

The beast slammed within him, desperate to come out. Would it be so bad if he let him out for a while? He couldn't let anything happen to Rebecca. If his wolf hurt her, he wouldn't be able to live with himself. She was his mate, destined to belong to him.

Without her, he was nothing.

There would be no point in living, in leading.

Running his fingers through his hair, he tried to think of something, anything that could help him. He couldn't bring himself to deal with this.

All of his focus was on his missing mate.

No, not missing.

Taken.

She'd been taken from him.

This was to make him pay.

To take his life.

"I've got to go and get her back," Liam said.

"If you do that, it's a guaranteed death sentence," Jake said. "We can't let you risk that. There's no way any of us could lead our people. You're an alpha, Liam."

"Right now, I'm a fucking mate. I've had mine taken from me. Try to imagine that kind of pain. I can't think right now, nor do I care about anything else other than getting her back. Don't you see that?"

"He's right," Eli said. "We'd all be doing the same. She's his mate. He needs her. We all need our women."

"But we also need him. If Liam goes, it gives Payne the opening he needs to take this pack, this land. You know what he's like. He's unstable. I get that Rebecca's not here and the danger she's in. We will get her back. I feel your pain, Alpha, but understand this, I'm part of this pack. As is my mate. I don't want her to be in any danger. You know what Payne is like. What he does to mates. He takes each mate for himself and impregnates them. It's why he doesn't have many followers. Why shifters have tried to leave him. He's brutal and brings death to his packs. I can't allow that to happen. So yeah, I've got to stop you from putting your life in danger, and you've got to come up with a plan. A good plan," Jake said.

The fear, the panic, he scented it. The wolf within him calmed enough to make sense of what was happening. His pack needed him. His female needed him. There was so much fucking need going around that he felt sick to his stomach.

It wasn't in him to sit and plan, but to act.

Taking a deep breath, he clenched his hands into fists and tried to calm himself. He didn't know what to do or what to say.

Breathe in. Breathe out.

"Please, Liam. I know you want her back. We'll help you every step of the way, but don't let anything happen to you," Jake said.

"I'm all for you attacking Payne, taking him out for good, but right now, you know you're running into a trap and I can't let you do that," Ben said.

Eli nodded. "I'm in agreement."

"Then what do you suggest?"

Jake breathed out a sigh of relief. "For a second there I thought your alpha wolf was going to attack us. They're going to expect you to go to her. Straight to her. We can follow any trail, Eli, Ben, and I. We have her scent. We can follow it."

"So?"

"You don't have to follow us. You don't have to go straight to her. You can lure them out yourself."

"They won't expect us," Ben said.

Liam paced.

Any mated male would go straight into the heart of danger without any thought. He wasn't *just* a mate though. He was also an alpha. Every instinct within him screamed to go and protect her. Without his friends, he'd have surely been dead by now.

"So we follow the scent. It'll put us on Payne's land," Liam said. "His pack is dying. There's not many men or women, and those that are there, are leaving." It was known that when pack members started to leave, it was only a matter of time before the strength within the pack slowly began to die.

Payne's leadership had pushed members out. He'd killed them. Damaged them from the inside out.

He was trying to take over another pack, to rebuild fresh, but his methods would produce the same results over and over. Every single pack he tried to take, would die from within. In the end, it would all be the same.

Someone had to stop him.

Glancing over at Alphie, Liam sensed the pain in his dog but also how sorry he was. Alphie adored Rebecca. Liam loved her.

We've got to go and get her.

"Fine." He headed toward the door. "Any sign of trouble, you leave and get the pack to leave as well. I won't have any of my people hurt at the hands of a man like Payne, understood?" Liam asked.

Ben, Eli, and Jake all nodded.

Leaving his home, he saw their mates waiting for them. There were tears and concern in the eyes of the three females. Liam watched as his men went to them and held each other close.

Rebecca should be home.

She should be meeting the other females.

He had to go and save her.

"We want to help," said Sarah, Eli's mate.

"Then please, get everyone ready," Liam said. "If I make it home and bring my mate, I know it's going to be a difficult time for her. This is all going to be new."

He looked at the women. "Would you go to Rebecca's home? She's human, and she'll be scared and worried, and I know this is all going to come as a shock to her."

"She doesn't know about mates?" Emily asked, Jake's mate.

"No. She doesn't know about any of this." He'd wanted to tell her, but Rebecca wasn't part of a pack. She loved wolves, but that didn't for a single second mean she would ever understand. This was his fault. His mistake. He wouldn't let anything happen to her because of him. "I'm not going to be able to let her go back. She'll have to stay here. Please, when you know all is well, could you go to her home? Get her things. Everything that you think will make her comfortable."

Emily nodded. "We'll do all of that. We're stronger than you think."

He nodded and stepped away, allowing his friends to say their goodbyes.

This was dangerous.

He wanted to send them home, to make them wait.

But that would put them at risk.

Staring into the forest, he thought about Payne. They'd had a couple of run-ins before. He'd always been the stronger and faster one out of the two of them. Now Payne thought he could take Liam's mate and that would be the end of it.

A rage built inside him thinking about what Payne had done. Not only had he taken his mate from him, he'd let her know exactly what he was, and not given him the chance to do it himself. For that, he would make sure Payne suffered horribly. That he'd want to die long before he granted it.

Liam was one to show mercy, to give people a second chance. Payne had crossed a line, and now he'd get to see just who he was dealing with. Liam had a reputation for getting the job done.

Payne would finally get what was coming to him.

****

Chained up.

Broken.

Alone.

Rebecca stared across the floor seeing a spider scurry away.

Even spiders didn't want to be near her.

She felt so empty.

So scared.

The fear gripped her, making it impossible for her to focus on anything else.

Wolves.

Real live wolves.

Not the kind that were in fairy tales and movies. They were real, and she'd seen it all with her own eyes. They'd had fun mocking her. Wiping the tears from her eyes, she sniffled. The man, Payne, had kicked her in the ribs with so much force, she'd slammed against the far wall.

She hurt everywhere, and her body shook from the cold.

Rebecca didn't even know how long she'd been taken.

Payne had been surprised, she knew that. He'd been expecting Liam to charge down and try to take her.

He'd not arrived.

They waited for hours, sitting around a dinner table.

Payne had mocked, laughed, and hurt her. Pinching her flesh, pulling her hair. Showing everyone that would listen just how weak she was. How useless. He'd even clawed at her neck where Liam was supposed to have marked her.

She placed a hand to the skin. It burned to the touch, and she wondered if wolves had infections. She was human, and if it was dirty, she'd be sure to die.

Death sounded all right now.

She'd rather be dead than have to deal with the truth that Liam had lied to her. He wasn't human, not completely. Half man, half wolf, and he'd lied to her. The mark on her neck, his need to take her. It hadn't been because of her. Well, it had and hadn't. He'd done so because his stupid wolf had told him to.

She wasn't attractive.

Or worthy of such a mate.

Payne had told her that.

Liam as an alpha needed someone strong.

Someone who could be worthy of his affections.

She was nothing.

In that moment, she missed her small apartment, her laptop, her authors, her work. She wanted to go back home. To forget about Liam, and the way he smiled or looked at her. It was all a lie, right? He didn't really have any feelings for her.

No one did.

"Aw, are we still alive?" Payne asked, giving her leg a nudge.

She flinched and tried to curl her body into herself, to make herself as small as possible.

It didn't work. She cried out as he grabbed her hair and pulled her up so that his cheek was against her own.

He'd stripped her of her clothing, and he'd made a point of sneering at her full body. Poking and prodding at her cellulite legs. Laughing at Liam's choice.

She couldn't handle much more pain or humiliation.

"Leave me alone. Please. I have nothing to do with this," she said.

"You have everything to do with this. You're the very reason we're here now, dealing with it. You're all the reason I need. Liam will come for you."

"He's not arrived. I'm not his mate."

"You are his mate, Rebecca. No matter what you say or how you try to hide it. You're his mate. He's a wolf, and I wouldn't be surprised if he hasn't tried to breed you yet."

The unprotected sex.

Payne burst out laughing. "So he has. Well, I have a good mind to keep you alive. Let's see if you have his baby. That would be fucking amazing. I kill Liam, take his pack, take his kid, breed you to bear my own children."

"I don't know who you are. Leave me alone." Her old anxieties were coming thick and fast. She wanted to run, but they had her chained up. She'd never been a fighter.

All she wanted was for Liam to come and save her, but he still hadn't shown up.

"You want to see the magic again?" Payne asked.

The sneer in his voice was clear even though she didn't look at him.

She shook her head, but that didn't stop him. Before her eyes, his arm changed from that of a human. She watched the skin split, disappear, and then in its place was that of a wolf. Dark black hair, long claws, and thicker than his human arm.

Screaming, she pushed at him, trying to scramble away, but she didn't get far. He grabbed her thigh, and she yelled in pain as his claws sank into the flesh. Glancing down, she saw the claws digging into her thigh. If she moved, he'd tear her leg to shreds.

"I've heard that human flesh is so damn easy. It's like cutting through paper."

She screamed once again as his claws moved the smallest distance. The pain rushed through her body, scaring her, terrifying her.

"You have so many delicate arteries and veins. You nick one and within minutes you've bled out and died."

Her heart started to pound. One of those was in her thigh. The femoral artery. She didn't want to die.

What did she want?

For this man to just be a bad dream and to wake up safely in her bed. It certainly felt like a living nightmare.

She held still as he continued to stare at her thigh.

"I'd love to watch you bleed out. I love the color red. So fucking sexy." His claws retracted, and she went to pull her leg against her, but he wouldn't let her.

Whimpering from the pain, she held herself still. His wolf hand was gone, replaced by his human hand.

"So delicate. I don't even see the appeal here. You're nothing. You're not worthy to have a wolf mate, let alone an alpha."

He stroked over the red wounds on her thigh now dripping blood.

This couldn't be where her life ended.

"Sir, something is happening," one of his men said.

Payne sighed. "He's taking way too long."

"You said he'd come for her. You think that would change? He'd change?"

"No. Liam is the kind of man who'd come back for her. I don't for a second believe he'd just leave her here." Payne sat back. "He's not like other wolves. First, he has a thing for dogs, which is just fucking gross. A wolf having a dog for a pet. It's insulting."

He always seemed to do a lot of talking.

"Right, I'll go and see what all the fuss is about. You, my sweet, are so much fun."

He walked away, and she watched him go as the door to her cage slammed shut. With him gone, she tried to pull her wrist free from the metal cuff he had around it.

She placed it between her legs, and then tried to pull, whimpering as the metal dug into the flesh.

Collapsing on the ground, she stared at her hand, feeling weak. Even if she was to escape, she was completely naked.

Where would she go?

They were wolves.

Actual wolves.

They'd track her down.

Kill her.

Tear her apart.

She closed her eyes and took several deep breaths. Everything was just happening too fast.

There was nothing she could do.

Closing her eyes, she saw Liam's smiling face. The way he'd watched her at the supermarket. The kindness he'd shown in helping her. Alphie by his side.

She hoped his dog was okay.

She loved that dog.

You love him as well.

She sniffled.

Even though Liam hadn't told her the truth, she couldn't stay mad at him. He'd gotten underneath her skin and helped her to realize what love was all about. She hadn't known him long, but she knew him long enough to know that she had feelings for him.

"What if I told you I'm fifty? Twenty years older

than you."

Everything made a lot more sense now. In a way, Liam *had* been trying to break the news of what he was to her. Asking her questions about wolves, her thoughts, her views. Anything that would help her get used to the thought of him being a wolf.

Was it so bad to think of him like that?

She was only at his home and the forest for a short time, but she'd felt that connection. With Liam, at his home, part of his pack, she'd felt at home. No place had ever felt like that to her. All of her life, she'd felt like the outsider, not really fitting in with anyone.

At least she got a taste of that just once.

You can't let go. Don't give up. Don't let them win. Fight. You're better than this, Rebecca. Stop being scared.

Liam will come.

He wasn't there.

He'll come.

You're his mate, and from all your reading on mates, he will come for you because he wants you, he loves you, and he'll hurt Payne. He'll protect you.

Opening her eyes, Rebecca sat up.

Taking a deep breath, she stared straight ahead.

She wouldn't give in or let them win.

She was stronger than this.

When Liam came, she'd be ready for him. When he got her home, he had a whole lot of explaining to do.

Chapter Nine

Of course, Rebecca hoped the commotion Payne went to check on was Liam coming to her rescue. It was a selfish thought, because as much as she wanted out of her prison, she didn't want Liam hurt. They were expecting him, and probably had some elaborate trap waiting, just like they'd used Alphie to entrap her.

She wasn't sure how much time passed, but one of the men walked by her cage, smoking a cigarette. He sneered at her. "Looks like we've got one of Liam's men. Won't be long until we have the rest, including the alpha." He blew out a cloud of smoke. "I suggest you get comfortable and settle in for the long haul."

Rebecca slunk, feeling boneless from the disappointment. Once alone again, she couldn't help but cry. Her life was a joke. Before meeting Liam, her daily life had been no different than living in this prison. She wished she'd been braver, taken more chances, but her damn anxiety always held her back.

Her arms cramped from holding them across her chest. No way would she give any of these creeps a free view of her nudity if she could help it. Even if they were grossed out by her rolls. The only man who mattered, the man who made her feel like a queen, was Liam.

"Hey."

Rebecca turned to the whisper. There was another naked woman on the other side of the bars. She wondered how many women were held captive here, but knowing she wasn't the only one made her feel less alone.

"Hi," Rebecca said.

The woman looked both ways, then stood up from her crouch. She had a gorgeous figure, the kind Rebecca could only dream of having. Her long, dark hair fell over both shoulders, partially covering her rounded breasts. She started picking the lock. What was going on? Was there a grand escape attempt? Rebecca didn't want to get hurt in the crossfire since she wasn't fast or stealthy.

When the lock opened, the woman pushed open the bars and curled a finger for Rebecca to come. She held up her chains, showing her there was no escaping. Not for her. Instead of running away, the woman joined her in the cell and went to work at the locks around her wrists.

"Who are you?" asked Rebecca.

She smiled, no sense of fear surrounding her despite their predicament. In fact, her confidence was palpable. "My name's Lilla. I'm Ben's mate."

Her mouth fell open. Ben was one of Liam's friends. One of his pack. "I don't understand."

The locks opened one after the other, and Rebecca was free. "Males can be hotheaded at times, especially when mates are involved. Sometimes they underestimate us, think we need their protection." She winked. "But she-wolves can be just as lethal. And we don't like to be told what to do."

She pulled Rebecca up to her feet.

"We'll never get out of here. There are so many men working for Payne. He could be back at any second."

What if something happened to Lilla because of her? This wasn't her fight, and Rebecca didn't want to be responsible for anything that could go wrong.

"We'll be fine."

"Lilla, I'm not a she-wolf. I'm human."

"I know. Come on." Just as they took their first steps, that asshole with the cigarette appeared around the corner and caught sight of them. He stopped dead, crushed his cigarette under his boot, then cracked his knuckles. Within moments, Lilla shifted into a snarling beast, her deadly fangs and intent gaze focused on the man. She lunged forward, sinking her teeth into his leg and shaking back and forth. When he cried out in pain, she knocked him down and went for his jugular.

It was over in seconds.

Blood pooled on the concrete, spreading around the body in a morbid display.

Rebecca stood in shock until the wolf let out a low bark to catch her attention. She knew Lilla wanted her to follow, so she stepped around the dead man and chased after the magnificent black wolf.

They weaved in and out of a tent camp, makeshift shelters and huts, barbeque pits, and clothes hanging on lines. Rebecca grabbed a white t-shirt off a line as she tried to keep up with the she-wolf, pulling it on over her head. It was long, covering just past her ass, and she instantly felt better despite her life still being in danger.

The wolf came to a standstill just ahead, the area sheltered by pines. Rebecca had never seen a wolf shifter in the fur. Part of her still felt a sliver of fear even though she knew it was Lilla under there somewhere. She was a beautiful animal, sleek fur, expressive eyes.

Lilla changed back into a human, morphing before her eyes. Rebecca would never get used to it, no matter how many times she witnessed such a miracle.

"Okay, you'll be safe here for now," said Lilla.

"Where's Liam?"

"The males had some plan in mind, but it fell apart when Ben was captured."

"Your mate?"

She nodded. "I'm going to save his ass, and then we'll all get out of here. Sarah is scouting the area. She'll come for you first. She's a white wolf." Lilla put a hand on Rebecca's shoulder. "Don't be afraid."

"I'll try my best."

"No, really, they smell fear. Think good thoughts, and we'll be back for you." She bent forward and landed on wolf feet. Before Rebecca could blink, there was no sign of the black she-wolf. She rubbed her arms, hating everything about the situation.

As time ticked by, she wondered if Payne had been right. Maybe Rebecca wasn't worthy of Liam. After seeing Lilla, her power, strength, and beauty, there was no way she could compare.

Stop it, Rebecca. These negative thoughts aren't helping anyone. Liam loves you, nobody else.

Then where was he? What if he was captured like Ben? Imagining something happening to Liam made her realize just how much she loved him. Love, such a big word. She'd only known him a short time, but the feeling was strong within her, leaving no doubt in her mind. Man or werewolf, it shouldn't matter. It didn't matter. She just needed him back.

She'd been kneeling on the forest floor for a while, not wanting her bare ass against the leaves and dirt. The white wolf she'd been waiting for came rushing by. It stopped dead, nudging her with its snout until Rebecca toppled over, and then it ran away. Another wolf raced by moments later, in hot pursuit of the beautiful white wolf.

A burst of emotion made Rebecca's sinuses sting. The wolf had saved her, knocked her down to hide from Payne's man. She prayed Sarah would be okay, that's she'd be able to outrun the enemy.

Who would come for her now?

Rebecca wasn't going to sit in the forest until nightfall. Everything was changing, and she had to be proactive. She crept back through the shacks and tents, listening and hiding. Her heart raced like a freight train, fear of being caught terrifying her. As she got closer to her original prison, she heard a yelp. The sound traveled straight through her, feeling like a punch to her gut. She peered through some knots in the boards of a ramshackle fence and saw red across the white wolf's fur. Rebecca gasped, covering her face and nose with her hands.

The black wolf was there, too, an iron collar around its neck. It thrashed and growled, despite being prodded with some kind of electric rod.

"How cute. They send their females to do their bidding now," said Payne. He turned and shouted into the forest. "How low will you go, Liam? I suggest you show yourself before nightfall or I'll be breeding your female." He laughed, the other men following his lead. When they found out she wasn't in her cell, it wasn't going to go over well. Their wolves would hunt her down easily, especially since she couldn't hide her fear.

"What do you want us to do with these?" One of the men pointed to the she-wolves.

Payne paced back and forth. "Lock them up for now." The white wolf managed to knock down one of her captors, even with her injuries. The she-wolves were truly impressive and fearless. "If Liam doesn't show up by tonight, kill them. His mate is the most important."

Rebecca shook her head. No, this couldn't be happening.

An arm wrapped around her waist from behind, and a hand came over her mouth just before she could scream. She kicked and struggled for all she was worth. Until she heard his voice.

"It's me, baby."

Rebecca whirled around, patting Liam down to ensure what she saw wasn't a figment of her imagination. His body was solid, heavily packed with muscle, and beyond human. "You came."

"Of course I came. Protecting you is my thing, remember? Trouble seems to follow you everywhere you go."

She wrapped her arms around his neck, savoring his heat, his strength, his presence. God, she loved him. "Please don't leave me. I'm so scared."

He tilted her chin up, kissing her on the lips, deeply, urgently. She closed her eyes and fell under his spell. "We have a plan. Ben let them catch him. It threw them off."

"The she-wolves are here. They're hurt."

Liam's chest rumbled. "They were supposed to stay behind. Jake and Eli will be sure to get them to safety."

"And me?"

He pulled her tight to his body, his big, rough hand grabbing her bare ass cheek. "When this is all done, I'm going to claim this ass. Every part of you will be mine."

Her pussy clenched. The deep, possessive tone of his voice made her clit ache for him. "Yes," she said. He kissed her neck where his mark was, then growled when he saw the damage caused by Payne.

"What else has that bastard done to you?"

She looked down at her thigh. Liam squatted in front of her, examining the cuts. He kissed them, his lips moving higher until he licked her pussy folds. She grabbed handfuls of his hair, but he shoved his tongue in her cunt while holding her ass. "Liam…"

****

Liam reluctantly pulled away from his woman. He'd been so worried, and all he could think about was loving her, mating her. When he saw her injuries, his anger for Payne only grew tenfold. That fucker was going to pay. Liam was going to ensure he suffered for harming his woman, his dog, and his packmates. Enough was enough.

"Stay here. Don't move. I'll be coming right back for you," he said.

She grabbed his arm. "Don't leave me. Please."

He cupped her cheek and kissed her once on the lips. Her big green eyes shimmered with unshed tears. "I'm here now. Nothing bad will happen to you."

"What if something happens to *you*?"

He chuckled. "That's not going to happen." Liam loved how she cared about him, but there was no need to worry. He knew damn well that even on his worst day he could defeat Payne. Today he was fueled with revenge, his alpha wolf raring to go. His only concern was controlling his wolf once he let it loose.

Would he be able to settle his alpha beast after unleashing it against his enemies? Jake told him their wolves would never harm their mates, but Rebecca was human, so no one knew for sure.

"Stay quiet. If anything happens, call for me and I'll be here." He disappeared into the forest before shifting. Liam wasn't ready to introduce her to his wolf, and not sure if he ever would be. He knew his identity had been exposed. She knew he was a werewolf, yet she still appeared to want him. Or was it just the protection she craved?

He dashed through the underbrush, barely disturbing a leaf. His packmates' thoughts were in his head. Eli had just released Ben. Jake was going for the she-wolves.

Liam insisted on handling Payne.

He broke the necks of two wolves doing perimeter recon. The taste of blood fueled his wolf. His fangs were bared and his muscles tense as he appeared in the clearing.

Payne's men fanned out around him, some in fur, some still in their human skin.

"About time. I thought you'd run off with your tail between your legs," said Payne. Liam didn't move. He focused his attention on his surroundings, the scents, and his enemy. "And your mate. Were the pickings that slim? I mean, come on, even by human standards I'd give her a failing grade. Of course, maybe you're into fat chicks."

He growled and flashed his fangs. Liam knew Payne was trying to provoke him, to throw him off his game, but it was still hard to listen to him insult his queen. He couldn't wait to rip him to shreds.

The thoughts in his head stole his attention briefly. His packmates were all free, and the she-wolves had been released. There was nothing Payne could use as leverage now, so it was time to take him down.

He leapt up against the human with a weapon in his hand, his massive wolf knocking him to his back. In one bite, he broke his neck. Why wasn't Payne more concerned? He was about to charge the wolf closest to him, when Payne tutted.

"I wouldn't do that if I were you. Unless you wanted to trade in your mate for a better model."

They didn't have Rebecca. She was safely out of sight, waiting for him to bring her to their home. Payne probably thought she was still locked in his prison, so Liam would use that to his advantage.

He took down the nearest wolf, ripping into flesh and bone, before tossing the carcass.

"I warned you." Payne jutted his chin, and one of his men came from the shelters behind him, Rebecca locked in his arms.

How the fuck had they found her so fast?

"You're probably wondering how we found your mate." He held up a small hand-held device. "They use these things for tracking pets. Microchipping or some shit. Came in handy today."

That piece of shit had microchipped his woman? Liam didn't want Rebecca to witness the carnage, but his alpha wolf was done playing nice. He barreled toward Payne, knocking his men aside in the process.

Jake and Eli were on the scene with Lilla. Sarah had been injured, and Emily was with child and was likely back at the homestead. They all fanned through the clearing, fighting, killing, decimating the enemy pack.

When Rebecca cried out, his wolf turned its attention to her. Power flooded his veins as the male holding her put pressure on her neck. Without her, there was nothing to live for.

He changed course, his mate's safety more important than revenge, more important than everything. Liam stopped dead in front of Rebecca. His chest heaved, his adrenaline flooding his system with energy and strength.

"Stay back or I'll snap her neck."

Liam had to make his next move carefully. His human woman was fragile, body and mind. A rash choice could get her killed.

"I'm not your pawn," Rebecca shouted, stomping her foot down on the male's. The moment of distraction was enough for Liam to bolt forward and latch onto the man's arm, tearing him away from Rebecca. She fell to her ass, leaning back on her elbows as she watching him bite the man over and over, long past his death. No one touched his woman and got out alive. Every one of these fuckers had a death sentence waiting for them.

He took slow, measured steps towards Rebecca, not trusting his wolf. She had on no panties, and he could smell her heat. Hear the blood flowing through her veins. He moved closer, sniffing her. When he found his love bite at her neck, his wolf and man merged, and his mind grew clearer. Human or not, Jake was right. He could never harm his mate.

Liam licked her mark, and she reached out and sank her hands into his thick black fur.

"I can't believe this is you."

He'd been so worried about rejection that he never stopped to consider she could be okay with his secret.

"Liam, watch out!"

He turned his head as Payne brought down a machete, striking him in the haunch. The pain only spurred him on. He whirled around, his hulking wolf taking down his enemy. Payne shifted into his grey wolf, and they tussled on the forest floor. The earth rumbled beneath them as they battled, slamming each other and striking out with fangs and claws.

He noted Lilla leading Rebecca away from danger, so he could let loose. His men waited on the periphery, and they wouldn't interfere in an alpha battle unless asked to do so.

"You're a monster, Payne. A worthless little shit."

"And you're going to lose."

Their growls and snarling kept everyone away. They had a wide circle of space where they clashed, violently attacking, their wolves taking extreme punishment. But Liam knew he had to end this. Payne was evil, and he wouldn't stop until Rebecca was his and he'd destroyed everything good in the shifter population.

Liam rolled to his back, feigning injury. When Payne leaped atop him, he went for the jugular, sinking in hard and deep, ensuring there was no coming back from this wound. As the other wolf's life ebbed away, the taste of his blood flooding Liam's mouth, he flipped up to his feet and looked down at his enemy.

It was over.

Payne would never hurt Rebecca again.

Liam shifted into his human form, and when he looked down his skin was covered in blood, some his, most of it Payne's. He was tired, strung tight, and needed the comfort he could only find with one woman.

She was standing in the near distance with Lilla. Her mouth was slightly open. Was that shock or fear in her eyes? He didn't want her to hate him, to be disgusted by what he was.

He didn't approach her, not wanting to scare her.

Rebecca took slow, robotic steps toward him. When she was within arm's length, her scent enveloped him. "Are you afraid?"

She licked her lips. "Numb."

"My wolf likes you." He ran the backs of his fingers along her cheek, loving every single thing about her.

"I like your wolf."

His beast howled within, and all was right in his world.

Chapter Ten

Several days later

Rebecca stared out of the window at the beautiful forest beyond. Liam had been spending a lot of his time either making her tea, dinner, or patrolling the perimeter. They hadn't exactly had a good talk since he saved her from his enemy Payne. At night, he wouldn't come in until he thought she was asleep.

She'd pretend as she knew he found it all a little difficult to talk about. The thing was, he'd bring her tea, they'd eat lunch, and she saw the hunger he had for her in his eyes. She felt that same exact hunger herself. No matter how much he wanted to deny it, there was no getting away from what they shared.

He was a wolf.

An alpha of a pack.

A pack of wolves that were really nice and sweet to her. They were like a family she never had. They were perfect, and she loved them all.

Finding out Liam was a wolf and alpha was … strange. Worse than strange. She'd been scared. Seeing him, being near him, that took all the fear and pain away and left only one thing, love. She loved him with all of her heart. The wolf and every single part that made him Liam. It didn't matter to her who he was or what he was.

To her, he'd always be the love of her life.

Her savior.

She heard the spoon stirring inside the cup. He was lingering way too long on making a cup of tea, and she found it irritating. This wasn't what she wanted.

She'd already come to terms with his wolf side and now she wanted him to come back to her and for them to be a couple again. This living in limbo, in awkward silence, wasn't going to work.

Holding the pillow against her stomach, she watched the world pass by. He knocked on the door, and she was so tempted to throw the pillow at him just to shock him or to jolt him out of whatever stupor he seemed to be in.

"Hey," he said.

Gritting her teeth, she forced a smile. "Hey."

Staring at him, she waited for whatever it was he was going to say. He just kept on staring at her.

"More tea, yay."

"You don't like tea?"

"I love tea."

"What's the problem?"

"I don't have a problem."

"I can sense that you have an issue, Rebecca. Out with it."

He stepped into the room, holding that cup in front of him, and she didn't know what happened. Her emotions were all over the place. She threw the pillow, even though she really didn't want to.

"You are my problem!" she yelled.

Getting to her feet, she charged over to him. He still held the cup and was staring at her in shock.

His shoulders drooped, and she didn't get it. "I'm sorry for all the pain that I've caused you." He set the cup on the side table.

She shook her head. "No. This is not about the pain or Payne either for that matter. This is about you and me. About the fact that you're always avoiding me. You won't hold me in your arms or love me or do or say anything. You're always out of the house. Do you even want me anymore, or have I become tainted because that … man-beast thing, ruined everything?"

"How could you even think that?"

"I could be walking around butt naked and you

wouldn't show an interest." Her cheeks were on fire right now.

"You just found out I'm a wolf. I'm being considerate here."

She blew a raspberry. She was so damn angry, and she couldn't believe that she'd just blown a raspberry at him.

Her body felt on fire.

He kept denying her, leaving her alone, and now she was at her wits' end. She didn't know what to do or say to make him see any kind of sense.

"You know what, I don't want to have this conversation."

"You cannot just blow a raspberry and leave!"

"I can do whatever the hell I like because you've done nothing but leave me alone. That no longer makes you my boyfriend or my mate. If you were either of those things, you wouldn't get to leave me, not once."

She brushed past him, heading straight toward the door, but he caught her arm.

"I love you, Rebecca," he said. "You're human. You're not used to having wolves around you or being part of a pack. I didn't want you to find out the truth this way, far from it. I love you more than anything else in this world. You being taken, it destroyed me. I failed you."

She saw the pain in his eyes as well as the fear. "You saved me."

"That asshole hurt you."

"And I'm healing. I'm not going to let him come between us, Liam. You shouldn't either. Otherwise he's won. We're better than that." She cupped his face, finally touching him after so long of not being allowed.

She pressed her head against his and breathed a sigh of relief. He was here.

He was listening to her.

They were home.

This felt like home.

"I don't want to leave."

"My wolf?"

"I'm not afraid of your wolf, Liam. I think he's beautiful, just like you. I don't want you to pretend to be something you're not. I'm here. I'm not going anywhere." She went up on her tiptoes and kissed him. "Make love to me, Liam. Fuck me. Have your way with me. I don't care what you need me to say. Just know that I love you, and I want you more than anything else."

He cupped her ass, drawing her close. "You mean like this?"

"Yes." Running her hands down his body, she cupped his rock-hard cock. "And with how this feels, I guess you want the same?"

"I never stopped wanting you, Rebecca. That has never been a problem with you. You're an addiction I don't want to stop."

Wrapping her arms around his neck, she pulled his head down, kissing him hard. Her body came alive under his touch.

He lifted her up, and she held him tight. He moved them through his home until they got to his bedroom. When he dropped her onto the bed, she stared up at him as he removed his shirt. Need unlike anything she'd ever felt consumed her. His hard, rough body was the ultimate temptation.

"You're my mate now, Rebecca."

"Just as you're mine." She felt possessive of him. He belonged to her in every single way.

"Always. I'm yours." He tore at her clothes, and she did the same to him, getting them both completely naked.

"I want my baby inside you, Rebecca. Tonight, I don't want to stop until I know I've bred you."

Those words should turn her off, but they had the opposite effect. Her clit ached, her entire body quivering with need.

She wrapped her fingers around his dick, working the tip into her mouth.

He groaned, and she smiled.

"Before you *breed* me, I want you to do something else."

He combed his fingers in her hair. "Anything."

"I want you to take my ass. I'll be completely yours, every single part of me." She didn't know what came over her, only that she couldn't stop the demand the moment it left her lips. Rebecca needed dirty, needed Liam to own her in every way.

He pulled her up and claimed her lips, pressing her to the bed. His chest rumbled, and the resulting growl nearly made her come.

She cried out his name as he kissed down her body, licking and sucking at her breasts before moving to her pussy. She watched him spread her open, his tongue dancing across her clit, teasing her. She didn't want him to stop and knew there was no way she'd be able to last.

He slid down, plunging inside her pussy before pulling back and teasing her clit. She cried out his name as he sucked her into his mouth. She'd tried to hold off, but she came, her body shuddering violently. Still, she wasn't sated.

Liam wouldn't stop now, she knew that. He kept on teasing her pussy, driving her to a second orgasm, and only when she'd come down from that orgasm did he turn her over and lift her up to her knees.

"You stop me at any point."

"I'm not going to stop you." She'd read a lot of

anal scenes during her editing, and it was always something she wanted to try, her little kinky obsession.

Liam was the only man she wanted to be with. The only one she trusted never to hurt her.

He spread the cheeks of her ass wide, and she closed her eyes as he stroked her cream back, getting her nice and slick. It felt so good him touching her there. The electric sensations surprised her, traveling straight to her clit.

When the head of his cock pressed against her, she tensed up, and moaned. There was no way to stop it. She wanted to give herself over to him completely. It was about trust and showing him she wasn't afraid.

"It's okay. Relax, baby."

She did as he asked, and when he pushed his monster cock inside her, she moaned, a desperate sound. There was discomfort but also pleasure, which completely overrode any pain. The new, unique sensations took her by storm. She gripped the sheet beneath her as he sank to the hilt. His hands braced her hips, holding her in place. Liam eased in and out of her, and she pressed back against his cock. She wanted more. She didn't want him to stop but to keep on fucking her. To keep on taking more.

"So fucking beautiful," he said. "I love your ass."

He covered her body with his as he kissed her neck. He thrust in deep, fucking her, and she loved every second of it. She released little gasps, never feeling so full in her life. So completely taken.

"I'll never stop wanting you, Rebecca, or loving you. You're my entire world. There's no way I'd ever be able to live without you. I wouldn't want to."

"I love you, too, Liam. Every single part of you. The wolf and you. I don't want you to change for me, or to be anything different. I love you."

He pushed in deep, his cock pulsing inside her. Liam fucked her ass, and she loved being naughty with him, exploring her sexuality in new, filthy ways. Over and over, he pistoned inside her, the bed rocking.

"Come for me, baby." He reached around and teased her clit, a new pressure building. The dual stimulation pushed her over the edge, and she screamed as the most powerful orgasm exploded inside her. Liam came as she milked his cock

As the intensity eased, he slipped out and picked her up, carrying her through to the bathroom. He set her on the counter and ran them both a bath. The humidity in the room grew heavy, the rushing water the only sound.

"Did I hurt you at all?" He took her hand and led her to the tub. They eased in together, the water warm, soothing all her aches.

"I don't think I sounded hurt, do you?" She turned in his lap, straddled his waist, and wrapped her arms around his neck. His big, hard body continually amazed her. "Never do that to me again. I love every single part of you."

"What are we talking about?" he asked.

"You ignoring me and avoiding me. I don't like it, and you don't need to do it." She stared into his eyes and smiled. "What did you think I was talking about?"

"Sex. Maybe the anal."

She chuckled. "No, I wasn't talking about sex."

"You're really okay with the wolf?" he asked.

"More than okay with it. He helped to save me. So he's in my good books."

"You realize we're the same person, well, you know what I mean."

Rebecca kissed him.

He leaned back, holding her waist in his hands. "I want you to move in with me."

"I thought I already had."

"No, officially. I want to go and get the rest of your stuff. No more apartment. You're mine, and I want to take care of you. You and our baby."

"We may not have made one just yet."

He placed a hand to her stomach. "I wouldn't be too sure about that."

"But…"

"I didn't use protection any time that I've been with you."

She placed a hand over her stomach. "You mean?"

"I think you are. I've noticed you smelled a little different the past few days. I didn't want to alarm you."

Was she holding her breath? She was in shock. Rebecca wasn't fit to be a mother—or was she? "You've known all this time?"

"Well, not all this time."

"We're going to have a baby?"

"Yes, and I want lots of them. I want to fill this house with them. You think you can handle that?"

"With you by my side, absolutely."

He wrapped his arms around her and held her close. His lips took possession of hers, and she moaned, kissing him back with the same passion he showed her. She didn't lie to him. This was where she wanted to be.

This was home.

****

Five months later

"I don't like this," Rebecca said. "What if someone sees?"

"You need to relax. The doctor said so, and it's dark. The full moon is up, and you need to cool off. The heat isn't doing you any good." Liam removed his shirt and shorts, staring at his wife. She wore a giant dress that hid most of her body.

They had discovered just the other day that she wasn't having just one child. Nope, his woman was going to give him twins. Two boys.

He was so fucking happy and proud right now.

In the moonlight, his wedding band glinted up at him. He was a happily married man, expecting twins, and completely at peace.

Grabbing the bottom of her dress, he started to lift it up.

She put her hands out to stop him. "No. You'll see me naked."

"Baby, I was the one that did this to you. I want to see my wife, pregnant or not."

"I don't know."

"You're the sexiest woman alive. My mate. My beautiful, sexy mate." He ran his hands down her back, gripping the edge of the dress and then tore it open, throwing the discarded pieces of fabric to the ground.

"Liam!"

She went to cover her body, but he wasn't having that. She didn't need to hide from him. Taking hold of her hands, he held them away from her body. The light coming from the moon showed her body to perfection. Her rounded stomach was ripe with his children, and he couldn't ignore those massive tits. His cock hardened just looking at them.

"Please," she said.

"Look at me, baby. I love you."

He took one of her hands and placed it over his rock-hard cock. "This is what you do to me. You are sexy as fuck. There's no way in this world that you'll ever repulse me. You're perfect."

"You keep saying that."

"Because it's the truth." He led her toward the

lake.

The cool water touched his legs, and he helped her in. The last few months had been perfect to him.

His pack were out patrolling the borders to keep them safe, not that he expected any other threat. Payne had been taken care of, and anyone who tried to take his female again, wouldn't succeed. He'd fucking kill them.

She wrapped her arms around his neck, and he saw her pout. "My stomach is touching you."

"I love it."

In the past few weeks she'd gotten a little self-conscious about her body. She couldn't sit up. Their babies were growing so fast. Of course, she was also bigger as she was carrying two children. They were big babies, which came with a whole host of problems. He wasn't thinking about them now, but he was planning. There's no way he'd ever be able to handle his woman leaving his side. So her care and attention had become the priority of the pack.

They were all helping them during this pregnancy.

With her being a delicate human, he was so fucking scared, but he wasn't showing that.

"This feels really rather nice," she said, releasing a sigh.

She kept her arms wrapped around his neck, leaning back, and he watched her. Her juicy tits captured her attention, her nipples big and dusky.

His hunger for her had never stopped.

"I can feel what you want." She chuckled.

"I can't help it," he said. "You're the one for me."

"Is this how you imagined life together?"

"I didn't imagine anything, baby. For a long time, I didn't think I'd ever have the chance to find the woman for me, let alone get her pregnant, or marry her."

"It was the best day, going to that grocery store," she said. "I had always wanted someone like you."

"Like me?"

"Who didn't care that I was ... strange."

"You're not strange."

"I've been thinking a lot lately," she said.

He waited, knowing it would be about the baby. She was constantly worried about every single detail, from giving birth to the babies not liking her, to everything in between. She'd decorated the room for the nursery three times in different colors. She kept changing the color scheme in case their sons didn't like it.

There was a stack of fifteen books by their bed, all to do with babies and pregnancy. He, himself, had read through plenty.

"And what have you thought?"

"That it doesn't matter if our babies love us."

"They will love us."

"I know I'm going to love our sons and all of our children with my whole heart. They'll hate me for a little bit, but that's what kids do, right? Hate their parents."

He smiled. "I won't let them hate you."

She cupped his face, kissing his lips. "Every time I'm with you, I feel like the luckiest woman alive. You gave me everything I could ever went, Liam. A family, a pack, a life, love, everything."

He held her close, kissing her, savoring his mate. Finally, he had his woman in his arms, and he couldn't be happier.

The End

BRED BY THE KING

Breeding Season, 4

Sam Crescent and Stacey Espino

Copyright © 2019

Chapter One

Ashley's heart raced as she ran as fast as her feet could carry her. She didn't know how much longer the group of men would be out, but she was determined to get away from them before they could rape her. No one was taking her against her will. She was thankful that they'd brought her to some kind of house where she'd been able to find the necessary ingredients to knock them out.

She pressed her body against the brick wall of an alleyway and took a second to catch her breath.

Her head hurt from being hit, and she felt sick to her stomach from being starved. Considering the population was at an all time low, she would have thought men would cherish the few females that were still alive. It seemed that was a joke.

Since a deadly virus had struck the world, people who had been weak or too young to make it had died. All of the scientists that had cooked it up, and the leaders who had unleashed it, were dead. In the few months since it had been released, chaos and war had broken out. Groups of men fought for land and survival. The women that hadn't been killed had been forced to be tagged based on their fertility status.

Once the virus had been unleashed, Ashley recalled all the women in her apartment block being rounded up. They had to go to a testing facility, and it was there that she received the tattoo on her wrist. It was a band etched into the skin by ink, which told the world who was fertile and who was not.

Ashley, for all of her luck, was fertile.

Yay.

Not.

In the beginning of being announced fertile, she'd been safe. The women who hadn't been so lucky had been forced back out into the world where no one gave a fuck. For her, she'd spent the first month in complete bliss and harmony. She'd been told she would be transported to a safe location where she would be put to good use, to aid humankind.

She knew what *good use* meant—bred. That was it.

She'd become nothing more than a vessel for a man's pleasure. At least, that's what they intended.

It never happened.

Before she even got a chance to be transported, the women had been taken hostage, and while the promise of death surrounded her, she made a run for it.

Rushing out onto the streets hadn't been her brightest idea, but at least she'd been able to finally be free. Only, it hadn't worked according to plan, either.

Men had seen her, seen the tag, and then she'd had to run for her life. She'd been doing okay until the latest group of men had hit her, knocking her unconscious and taking her to wherever the hell she was when she woke up.

She didn't recognize anything, and she kept trying not to freak out.

Getting away from them had been her lucky break. After the group of men had taken her, they'd told her they were all going to fuck her, to fill her womb so full of cum so that she would breed them more women to take as their own.

It had sickened her to the core.

Before the fucking could start though, they had demanded she feed them. So, using the ingredients around her, she'd fed them, but she had put in a few other ingredients as well. Especially the sleeping pills she'd found in the cupboard. She didn't know if crumbling them into their food would work, but she had used every single one in the hopes of getting away.

The moment they'd fallen asleep, she took off.

She couldn't stop. If she stopped, she'd be taken again. That prospect was not acceptable to her.

Staring down at the ink around her wrist, she gritted her teeth. At the time, she hadn't thought much about the fertility tattoo they'd forced her to wear. Now though, it had pissed her off. She felt like cattle. It amazed her how humankind could turn so savage in such a short frame of time.

Before all media outlets had gone down, a broadcast into what the bands signified had gone out to the world. Any woman found with the fertile band had to be taken to the government immediately.

Of course, that hadn't happened. When she saw the broadcast, she should have known something had fucked up.

Why would women who had the band be out in

the world?

They had the sense to run before it was too late.

Pushing down the sleeve of her jacket, she shook her head, hating herself for her own weakness. This was not what she wanted to do, but now her life was survival.

Stepping away from the wall, she began to follow a new path, no real destination in mind.

She knew it wasn't safe anywhere, so she was on alert.

One of the female scientists had sat with her for long hours and told her what was going on in the world. The virus that had been released caused the victims to have seizures and become violent before they died a painful death. They would go mad with a need for killing. The scientist said that they didn't know who exactly unleashed it, and there was no cure. It scared her to know someone could create something so evil.

The death toll had risen sharply, and as Ashley looked around the changed landscape of the world, she knew nothing would ever be the same again.

Folding her arms over her chest to keep out the chill, she made her way along a darkened street when she heard a feminine scream.

She paused, fear gripping her with its claws.

"Get off me!"

"That pussy is mine. All fucking mine. I want it. I want it."

Rounding the side of the building, she saw a man had a woman by the throat. His hand going to his pants, trying to pull out his dick. Lying near the wall was a pile of discarded rebar. Without thinking, she picked one up and slammed it against the man's head. That was all it took for him to go out cold.

The woman underneath him scrambled out.

Ashley dropped the metal and stepped away,

glancing down at her empty hand.

"Hey," the woman said, rushing to her side.

She stared at her.

"Thank you," the woman said.

"It's all right. Men shouldn't be hurting us," Ashley said.

"No, they shouldn't, but that doesn't mean they won't. Men have always been a law unto themselves."

"I've got to go." Ashley pulled away.

Just as she moved past her, the other woman grabbed her arm. It was the one that had the band around her wrist. Light cast down by the lamp, and the woman held her hand up.

"You're a fertile?"

Ashley pulled her hand away from the woman, hiding it behind her back. "I said I've got to go."

"Wait. It's too dangerous for someone like you."

"Someone like me?"

"I don't mean it as a negative. I mean that you're precious. What you can do is precious."

"I don't know what you're talking about." She just wanted to run away right now. Ashley wanted to be safe, invisible, not some precious breeding vessel.

"You're not going to make it," the woman said. "My name is Luanna. Look, I'm not going to hurt you. You think that's the first man that's tried to rape me?"

"I'm sorry about that."

"No, he's the first one that hasn't succeeded. He's not the first one to actually try and do it."

She saw Luanna's pain, and it scared her. Tears pricked at Ashley's eyes for the injustice of it all.

"I'm trying to get to Draven's Kingdom."

"Draven's Kingdom?" Ashley asked.

"Draven's this guy. Some people believe he's ex-military. I don't know what he is, but I know he's been able to make something out of this shithole. This world isn't safe for women, but I've heard he takes care of men, women, *and* children."

"Children? I thought they all died."

"Not all of them. Whatever the virus was, it preyed on the weak and vulnerable. Some kids, they're strong. I don't know what happened, but I know there are children living. Please, let me try to help you."

"You want to help me?" Ashley asked.

Luanna grabbed her wrist. "This, it makes you invaluable, but it also means that men will fight for you. They'll fight to keep you, and some may even use you."

"What makes you think this Draven will be any different?"

"I don't know, but I have hope. Don't you have hope?" Luanna asked. "What have you got to lose?"

Ashley rubbed the back of her head, thinking about the men who'd tried to rape her. There really was nothing to fight for anymore. She had no one. Nothing. The life she once knew was a thing of the past.

"Can you at least tell me your name?" Luanna asked.

"Ashley. My name's Ashley." She held her arm close to her chest. "I don't know what to do."

"Then let's go together. I don't know about you, but I'm out of friends right about now. We can take care of each other. It's better than going alone."

"You don't have one of these bands?"

"No. Only fertile women get those. I was tested and thrown out on the same day. Like trash."

"I'm so sorry."

"Don't be. I imagine it's not good for you either." Luanna held her hand out, and they locked their fingers together. They started to walk.

Ashley had learned that trust had to be earned

but, right now, she'd never felt so lost. She was going to take a leap of faith and hope Luanna didn't turn out like all the others.

It was the best thing she could do right now.

****

Draven drove his blade into the rapist that had tried to attack one of the females under his care. What he'd created wasn't much yet, but he had vowed to protect anyone within his walls.

He'd managed to create a safe haven within an old mansion estate that spread out across numerous acres of land. The entire property was surrounded by twelve-foot brick walls, a security gate, and the house had at least twenty-five bedrooms that he counted.

The moment the virus was released, he'd set out to make himself a safe place. The world quickly deteriorated to survival of the fittest. He planned to come out on top. This property had been ideal to start his safe haven. It was complete with a wine cellar, storage facility, and fields to grow food, not to mention the surrounding land under his guard.

The house was almost full, and some of the game rooms had been converted into bedrooms.

Most of the people who came to the house were alone. He was shocked when he saw his first woman and child.

He'd vowed to protect them, to keep mankind alive in a world full of death and destruction. Draven had come from a military family. As soon as he was of age, he'd joined. Before the world went to shit, he'd been an active Marine, and he'd seen his friends die. His tours had been in some of the worst war-torn countries, but they didn't compare with life after the virus.

Draven was particular about who he let in his walls. Trust wasn't something he gave easily. When he agreed to offer a man protection, they had to agree to look out for every person in their community.

He stood at the gate, staring down at the man whom he'd already injured. He was a traveler, just passing through, and Draven had been foolish enough to let him in.

Draven had been awoken in the middle of the night as this man had wandered into a woman's room and she'd been screaming for help.

His place was supposed to be safe. He'd promised the women they would be taken care of.

This man had nearly made him break his vow, had put his reputation at stake.

Death was the natural order of life. And he wasn't afraid to get blood on his hands to support his cause.

For a long time, he had fought for freedom and the chance for people to grow up in a safe place. He'd worn his uniform with pride. That had all changed when the first virus was released. He'd seen the land he loved so much torn apart. People changed, turned wicked in their desperation. The love he had, it was gone. He'd become hard, cruel, determined not to be a victim.

The land was a battleground for the strongest.

Those that couldn't survive would either die or become slaves to the men and women who captured them. But it didn't take long for him to realize not every human had turned evil. There were still good people out there, and his focus shifted from blind battle mode to the need to preserve the good left in the world.

Slashing the knife across the man's throat, he watched him bleed out, waiting until the life completely drained from his body.

"Let it be known now, if any of you think to take what is not freely given, you will face the same punishment. Women are not here for your fucking pleasure. They have a right to survive just like everyone else." He wiped the blade on the man's shirt and entered the gates.

He waited as the men who had assisted him stood over the man's body. Draven's following was loyal, but he'd never put one hundred percent faith in any man. His strength was only relying on himself.

Slowly, one by one, they entered the gates.

"What are you going to do about repopulation?" Luke asked.

Luke once had a wife and child, whom he'd lost on the same day. They all had a story to tell, and one day Draven intended to hear them all.

"You know the drill. No repopulation without women who are fertile," Draven said.

"But we know some are," Benjamin said. "That broadcast. It told us what to do if we find a female wearing a distinctive band."

Draven laughed. "You think they're going to allow those women out to anyone? They're going to be for the rich, the wealthy. The men in high places. They'll probably be auctioned off to the highest bidder."

"Money doesn't buy anything."

"For us right now, it doesn't. We don't know what kind of currency there is. Just be happy that right now you've got a safe place to sleep, warm food, and someone to keep you company, which is a damn sight more than I can say for a lot of people."

With that, he entered the mansion. He didn't stop to make small talk with any of the women who had been vying for his attention. Everyone was looking for power in one form or another.

He wasn't interested in sex, or in anything but surviving. Death would come for them all. But he didn't intend to go easily.

He walked up to the loft, pulled down the stairs, and entered the roof through the small door. He made his way toward the edge and looked all around.

There were a few garden pots lying all around, and he imagined they once belonged to a gardener or maybe a wife in the house, or someone who liked roof gardening.

The plants were all dying anyway.

Running a hand down his face, he took several deep breaths and stared up at the night sky. It had been nearly a year since the virus was unleashed.

He sat on the edge of the roof for the longest time, lost in thought, feeling alone even though the house was full. He watched the sun start to rise, sleep once again failing him. He'd not slept a lot in recent weeks. He didn't like the uneasy feeling that kept him up at night.

Having been on the front lines, he knew that more trouble was coming.

What he wanted to know was how bad and when it was coming. He had to be prepared, to protect what he'd created here.

With the sun finally up, he got to his feet and left the safety of the rooftop, heading back down to the main kitchen.

"It could be worse," Anna said. She was one of the few women who'd come for sanctuary.

"How could what be worse?" he asked, entering the kitchen.

He saw at least ten people were already down for breakfast. The coffee was on. The one good thing about this place, there seemed to be an endless supply of coffee and food. He wondered if the person who once lived here was a doomsdayer, the kind of person to prepare for a potential apocalypse.

"Our situation. I mean, yeah, it's bad. Our population has dwindled, and a lot of people have died. There's no active government or head of state, but I mean, at least the people who are dead are not coming back to eat our brains."

"She thinks that because there are no zombies around, we're all good," Luke said.

"Hey, it's not funny. I'm being serious," Anna said.

"So am I. There's nothing about our situation that's good."

"I don't know, I'm glad we don't have a couple billion people knocking at the gate wanting to suck our brains out," Draven said. "That's a plus."

He took a sip of his coffee and tried to hide the disgust. Whoever had made it couldn't make coffee.

"See, I told you."

"Draven, we've got company," Benjamin said, coming into the kitchen.

Everyone tensed.

"What kind?"

"Two women. They look tired."

Draven reached for his gun. The men followed him out, and they all approached the gate. He held the gun up. It wouldn't be the first time a gang had tried to take his land by using a woman as bait. He had no interest in finding out if that was the case now.

"Whoa, whoa," one of the women said.

The other one remained quiet. Her wide blue eyes stared at the gun in his hand.

"We don't take in just any strays. You're alone?" Draven asked.

"I want to make sure this is Draven's Kingdom."

"What?" He didn't have a name for his place, but hearing that, it was weird.

"Ashley and I, we're looking for Draven."

He assumed the sexy blonde was Ashley.

"You're looking at him."

"Really?"

"Yes. Now, what the fuck do you want?"

"I'm Luanna. This is Ashley. We need a place to stay. We can earn our keep. I promise you. We've been traveling all week, and look, she's a fertile."

Before Ashley could stop her, Luanna had grabbed her wrist and showed them the status marking.

The men took a step closer, but Draven saw the fear in Ashley's eyes. She jerked away from her friend, her loose bun coming undone. Damn, she sparked something inside of him.

Luanna had no right exposing her friend, but he also couldn't allow the two women to leave his premises now.

"Open the gate," he said, giving the order.

Like always, the gate was only opened a short distance, just in case someone decided to try to sneak in or to ram it open.

He pushed his way through the men and went straight to Ashley, who kept backing up until the closed gate stopped her.

"Please don't hurt me," she said.

He reached down, grabbing her wrist and inspecting the band that declared her as fertile.

"Welcome," he said.

Chapter Two

Draven never gave much thought to the fertile women the government claimed were running loose, a huge bounty on their heads. He considered them more a tall tale, a story people shared to give them a bit of hope.

He'd never seen one in the flesh. If the virus didn't kill them, it rendered most women infertile. The moment he saw that tattoo on Ashley's wrist, something came alive in him. The prospect of continuing life, of creating a new world excited him. It was more than that. The girl with the long blonde hair had an air of innocence that pulled him in.

She'd be his.

This was his kingdom, and even though most of the women within the walls hoped he'd choose them as a mate, he'd had no interest in any woman—until today.

He tucked his gun into the back of his jeans and held out his arm so the women would feel welcome to enter the main yard of the property. They moved tentatively, easily jumpy. He wondered what they had been through.

"Are you hungry?" he asked. They both turned to him at once. Luanna nodded eagerly, but Ashley just stared at him. He approached her, tilting her chin up with a curled finger. "I asked you a question."

She swallowed hard, but kept quiet. Feisty or terrified, he wasn't sure. Either way, just being near Ashley made his cock hard. It had been over a year since he'd fucked a woman, and right now that fact was making itself painfully clear. Somehow, even being starved, she'd managed to keep her lush curves. Her jacket barely concealed the fact she had huge, sloppy tits. So many of the women who came through these gates were emaciated, not unlike Luanna.

"Yes, she's hungry, too," Luanna answered for her.

He brushed the hair from Ashley's forehead. Even with all the dust and smears of mud, she was still the most breathtaking thing he'd ever seen. The loneliness that had plagued him the past year suddenly felt irrelevant. His focus shifted.

Draven wasn't sure how long he'd been standing there, staring at Ashley, but Luke cleared his throat to snap him out of it.

"Boss?"

"Right." He took a step back, taking a cleansing breath. "Bring them to the kitchen, feed them well, then get them cleaned up. New clothes, too," said Draven.

"Are they going to be staying on?" asked Luke. They often aided travelers, then sent them on their way. They couldn't house every person passing through or they'd be overrun and their supplies would be devastated. It was a hard world, and they had to make tough choices.

"Luanna can sleep in the women's dorm for now. Bring the fertile one to me after."

There was silence, and a couple gasps, but no one dared to challenge him. It was unlike him to show any interest in a woman. He stood rooted in place as the men ushered the newcomers forward to the kitchen. Ashley kept looking back over her shoulder at him. She was young and ripe, maybe early twenties, half his age. It didn't matter to him. For the first time in a long time, he cared about something beyond survival.

Draven's Kingdom. He played with the words in his head. He'd never really thought about his role in this world he'd created. Maybe king *was* an appropriate title. He licked his lips as he watched the jiggle in Ashley's ass. Fuck, she turned him on without even trying. He could already envision her naked, and all the filthy things he wanted to do to her body.

It didn't matter how long it took, she'd be bred by the king.

Benjamin came and stood beside him. "I thought you said no man living here could take without consent. Does that not include you?"

He clenched his jaw to contain his irritation. "I make the rules here, not you. Just worry about abiding by them, eh?"

"Yes, Boss."

"And don't worry about Ashley. When I take from her, she'll be more than willing. I can guarantee you that much," said Draven. "Make sure no one goes near her but me. I want her untouched."

Benjamin nodded, then joined the others.

Draven retired to his bedroom on the upper level, the largest master suite in the mansion. It overlooked the front courtyards and had its own grand bathroom done in the finest marbles. Back when he'd been serving in the military, he'd never had much in the way of material possessions. He traveled a lot, lived in different places, never really settling down.

This place, this kingdom, was growing on him. He savored the power, but he wasn't foolish enough to abuse it. This place was going to be different, and he'd fight to keep it that way. No corruption, no rapes, no murder. Whoever broke the rules, paid the ultimate price. It was just the way it had to be.

He'd seen what desperation, fear, hunger, and the thirst for power could do to a man—most men—since the virus was released. Draven could play their ruthless game. He wasn't afraid of what roamed outside his walls. In fact, he dared anyone to try to take his land. He'd developed a reputation for a reason. Any man who fucked with him would be made an example of.

Draven lay down on his bed, staring up at the ceiling. Yes, he craved Ashley in the most carnal ways, but it was more than the desire to fuck her. He wanted a partner, a queen. And the little fertile was the key to his future, *their* future. He could see it now, her stomach round with his child, his legacy.

A reason to live.

His protective instincts soared. No man would go near his prize. He sat up in the bed, anxiety creeping in. He didn't feel safe with such a treasure as Ashley out of his sight. Even his most loyal man could be tempted to steal a marked fertile away for the bounty promised by the government. Or to fill her with their own seed.

He was about to rush downstairs, when someone knocked on his door.

"Come."

The door opened, and Luke had his hand firmly around Ashley's upper arm. He gave her a shove into the room as she protested being restrained, brushing off her jacket once away from him. Her little scowl reminded him of an angry kitten.

"You wanted this one?" asked Luke.

Ashley wore new clothes, a slightly fitted blouse and long, flowing skirt. Her face was clear of grime, a cute spattering of freckles on her cheeks. That beautiful blonde hair was brushed smooth, falling around her like a shawl.

"She's a fertile. Why would I want the other one?"

He motioned for Luke to leave them alone. The other man closed the heavy wooden door behind him. Ashley turned and stared at the closed door. She stayed frozen in place, refusing to face him.

"Have you eaten?"

She tentatively turned around, as if being forced

to face a monster. Maybe she saw all men in a negative light. He'd have to change that with time.

"Cat got your tongue?"

She nodded. "I've eaten." Her voice was a soft, little whisper, pure sweetness and femininity. His claim on her grew tenfold. He noticed she kept rubbing her wrist, trying to conceal her mark with the other hand.

He got up and paced, his hands clasped behind his back. "How long have you been out there on the run?"

She shrugged. "I can't really remember. The days seem to blend into one another."

"Survival will do that to a person," he said. "That's over now. You're safe here. I'll protect you."

Ashley looked him in the eyes. "Why?"

He smirked. "I can't be a nice guy?"

"There's no such thing. Not anymore."

Draven tried to imagine the horrors she'd faced before showing up at his gates. He didn't even want to think of another man's hands on her, hurting her, taking when she didn't give freely. The world had hardened her, like so many others, and it would be a challenge to prove he wasn't a complete asshole.

"You've been through a lot. Tell me, Ashley, have you been violated by men while you were out there?"

She tensed, her body visibly stiffening. She shook her head.

"Are you sure about that?"

"Luanna has. A lot of women have. I guess I'm one of the lucky ones."

"Lucky for *me*."

****

Ashley wasn't sure what to feel, what to think. Her mind told her not to trust any man. Her body, on the other hand, wanted to give in. When Luanna had mentioned Draven and his kingdom, it had intrigued her. She never imagined such a place existed, and she certainly didn't imagine a king with tousled dark hair brushing his collar and eyes as dark as night. His size intimidated her, tall and thick with muscle. He carried himself with pride and confidence, maybe a bit of arrogance … and damn it turned her on.

He'd taken care of her, fed her, offered her safety and everything that had been taken from her. But it was all lies. He only wanted her because she was fertile, a rare commodity. Even though he was nice to look at, he only wanted her to become a baby-making factory, not unlike the remaining government sector she'd escaped from.

She wasn't an animal, a vessel to be bred.

What she wanted no longer existed. Love and family were things of the past, something for future history books. If only his narrowed gaze, the one perusing every inch of her body, saw something more than a fertile. If Ashley had to choose a man to love her, she wouldn't hesitate to select Draven. He was perfect—rugged and fearless, powerful, hypnotizing.

He came closer, and she instinctually backed away.

"Relax, little one. I said I won't hurt you."

There was a scar across his cheek, his thick stubble not growing along the seam. It only added to his appeal and intrigue. She caught his scent as he walked back and forth in front of her, a spicy sandalwood that she breathed in deeply.

"Sit down." He pointed to a loveseat near his bed. She complied, cautiously sitting on the floral print cushion. "Tell me about yourself. Before the virus. What did you do for a living?"

She cocked her head, confused by his question.

"People don't talk anymore. The art of conversation died with most of humanity, it seems. Tell me something. A memory. Anything."

Ashley swallowed hard. This was strange, almost dreamlike, but it took her focus away from basic instincts and allowed her to think back to when life had been normal. Sane.

"I was a nursing student. My last year." Her own voice sounded odd to her. "I had a dog. His name was—" Tears filled her eyes because she couldn't even remember. So much of her past had been blocked out, maybe for her own sanity.

"It's okay, baby." Draven squatted down in front of her, one hand on her knee. "It'll take time. Don't worry about it."

She took a deep breath, not wanting to appear weak in front of a man.

"Do you remember any of your hobbies?"

"Reading. I loved to read, but most of the books have been burned for heat," she said.

He smiled. "I have a library downstairs. Fully stocked. I'll show it to you later, if you like."

She couldn't help but smile back. Ashley wondered if her face would crack. It had been so long since she had something to smile about.

"It's good to keep the mind active. Sometimes an escape is vital these days, don't you agree?"

She nodded, trying not to stare at the broadness of his shoulders or the way the material of his shirt tightened around his biceps.

"Me, I was a Marine. Good one, too. Fought for freedom, or so they told me. Maybe I was a pawn for the government, an assassin for their greed. Who knows? Now, there's nothing worth fighting for." He wet his lips.

"No, that's not true. Not anymore." His hand was still on her knee, and she could feel his heat and every twitch of his fingers. Her core coiled tight, her reaction to this man unnerving her. "Do you have any fears, Ashley?"

She loved the way he said her name, like it was a dessert he was savoring.

"Men. Being a victim." Why was she opening up to this stranger? This had to be all an act. But somehow, he made her feel safe, her hard layers falling away. "I never asked to be a fertile, but it's a curse, not a blessing."

"Don't say that. It's a beautiful thing. A gift." His hand slid slightly higher, resting on the fleshy part of her thigh. Could he hear her heart pounding in her chest? It sounded deafening in her ears.

"That's because you're a man. You probably don't have any fears."

He scoffed. "I'm afraid of a lot of things. Some I never even realized until you showed up at my gates. Most of all, I'd say the biggest one is death."

This caught her interest. "Everyone has to die."

"The way the world is now, the next day is never a guarantee. I've seen so much death, even before the virus. I want no part of it."

"So you'll stay alive forever?"

He chuckled. "Maybe I will. What about you? Care to join me?"

She shrugged, playing along. This fairy tale was better than her reality for now.

"We can forget the rest of the world, stay here, and live forever. Just you and me." Something changed in his demeanor, a darkness passing over his features. Hunger. She wasn't afraid. If anything, she didn't trust her own instincts when it came to Draven.

Instead of giving in, of embracing his clear

seduction, she forced herself to smarten up. He only wanted what her body could give him. If she didn't have the fertile band, she wouldn't be sitting in front of him right now. "But then the story ends, and we wake up. There's no hiding from the truth."

He stood up, and part of her was disappointed he didn't try harder.

She watched as he walked over to his dresser, a finely crafted wooden piece of furniture with intricate carvings. Something that belonged to royalty. He picked up a book, and her heart leapt.

Draven walked around the massive room, occasionally peering out a window, holding the book to his chest. What was he thinking? Planning? A man like him was intelligent, carefully crafting every word before he spoke it.

When he finally returned to her, she held her breath in anticipation.

He sat beside her on the small loveseat this time, the cushions sinking slightly from his weight. His presence was pure masculinity. Draven held the book out to her, but when she attempted to take it, he pulled it away. She looked at him, confused, but saw the teasing quality in his eyes.

"Would you like to have a look at this book?"

She nodded, not sure what game he was playing.

"Okay, I'll trade you. One kiss and I'll let you read some of it."

It was a tempting offer, one she couldn't refuse on either count. But he should know what he was dealing with. Despite the state of the world, Ashley was a virgin. Inexperienced and terrified of losing her innocence to any man. She'd witnessed women being raped, and had to listen to Luanna's horrific recounts during their travels together.

"Just a kiss. I have nothing more to offer."

This appeared to pique his curiosity. "You have so much to give. We both do."

She shook her head. "If you're looking for someone to breed, you should keep looking. I didn't break free from the government's program just to be an experiment for you."

He leaned back slightly. "You've insulted me," he said.

Her heart raced, this time with a hint of fear. Had she crossed a line? Was he going to force her out of his protected little world?

"I didn't mean to."

"I've only taken care of you since you arrived, have I not? Have I hurt you? Threatened you in any way?"

"No," she whispered. "I'm sorry."

He paused. "Apology accepted. But I'm wondering. Are you not attracted to me?"

Her stupid body heated again, because he was so close and smelled so damn good. "Probably every woman is."

"I didn't ask you that, Ashley. I don't care about other women or their opinions. You're the one in my room. You're the one I've chosen for myself."

Did he really just say that?

Should she feel flattered or threatened? Being chosen made her feel wanted in a world out to destroy itself. Even before the virus, men often looked the other way because of her constant weight issues and often awkward shyness. It felt empowering for such a desirable man, a king no less, to choose her out of so many women.

"I'm a virgin," she blurted, half out of breath.

He tilted his head, a comical look twisting his

features for a second. "You're very jumpy. You need to relax." He brushed her hair behind her shoulder and ran the backs of his fingers over her cheek. She didn't dare move or breathe. "And don't worry about being a virgin. I'm a patient man, and I'm not against giving you lessons. Now, how about that kiss?"

Chapter Three

Draven watched as Ashley stared down at the book. Clearly, she wanted to read it, but she was also too nervous to trust him. He liked seeing her nervous, watching as she bit her lip and her cheeks blushed.

Her innocence shocked him to be honest. In this world of kill or be killed, the fact she'd remained a virgin was a miracle in itself.

"What do you mean, you've chosen me for yourself? You don't even know me."

"You're trying to avoid the kiss."

"I'm trying to stay alive." She held up her wrist. "This doesn't give any man a claim over me, regardless of attraction or not. I'm not some pawn to be used for your own amusement." She got to her feet, but he caught her wrist. His fingers banded around the ink that marked her as fertile.

Every single fertile woman had gotten this band. It marked them from all the other women. He could be with anyone else, and there were plenty of women in his kingdom that wanted him.

"You're safe here."

He put the book down but made no move for her to take it.

She snorted. "I'm safe? I'm here, and Luanna is not. I don't like this. I don't like any of this."

"Sit down." He made sure his voice didn't give her a chance to argue. She lowered herself into her seat. He released her hand, and she pulled her legs up around her, hugging them to her body.

"Now, you're safe here. The men follow me. You're a fertile woman, Ashley, and that means you're going to come with a certain want."

She shook her head. He couldn't deny it. He

wanted her, to spread those thighs and to have a taste of her virgin pussy. To tear through that virgin wall, make her his, and fill her with his child.

This world wasn't going to repair itself any time soon. They all had to make the most of what they wanted.

"Out there you will be nothing more than a vessel. A place for a guy to fuck and breed."

"That's what *you* want," she said, the accusation clear in her voice.

He got to his feet, trapping her in the chair she sat in as he hovered over her. There was nowhere for her to go. Compared to his sheer size she was nothing more than a slip of a woman. His training also put him ahead of most men.

She gritted her teeth, and he saw her taking deep breaths. Fear flashed in her eyes, but she quickly disguised it.

"I will protect and care for you, Ashley. All I ask is for a mere kiss so you can read the book. Is that so bad? Others would ask for far more."

She stared where he'd placed the book. So harmless.

All it would take was a kiss.

Men had never given her a reason to trust them, but maybe she was wrong this time. Could Draven be different? Was she judging him unfairly? It was hard to trust anyone anymore, let alone men. At least he hadn't attacked them.

"I won't hurt you. I'll take care of you." He stroked her cheek with the back of his fingers and hated how she flinched away. "I see we're going to have to work on that."

He took his seat again. Picking up the book, he held it in his hand. "I guess I'll have to prove to you that

I mean you no harm. Once I've done that and you've given me the kiss I want, I'll let you read it."

With that, he didn't say another word. He walked to the door, left the room, and flicked the lock into place.

"What are you doing? Let me out." She slammed her hands against the door, and he smiled. *Not a chance.*

He'd seen the hungry look in the other men's eyes when they caught sight of her. Being the strongest, the king, he got what he wanted, not his men.

Whistling to himself, he made his way back down to the main room. At the foot of the stairs sat Luanna, the woman that had been with Ashley.

She stood up the moment she caught sight of him. She was a pretty thing but nothing compared to Ashley.

"Why have you taken her?" Luanna asked.

"I'm going to keep her safe."

"I heard this place was a safe haven for women. That you protected us and yet, you take her and don't care about her own needs. I want her returned. We'll leave here and be out of your hair."

"That's not going to happen. You can leave by all means but not her."

"How dare you? You're not her father. You're nothing to her. She's not yours. She's her own person, not an animal."

"You want to take her out of this place. You think that's wise? You know what it's like to have your choice taken from you. To be raped. You want that same kind of life for her?"

"What are you doing to her now? You want her, and rather than give her time, you're going to rape her."

"I don't rape women."

"Then let me see her."

"No."

"You're a horrible man. Horrible, horrible man."

She stood in his way, and he found himself growing ever more bored with this conversation. "You done?"

"I don't know how anyone would want to follow such a vile person. Give me back Ashley."

She charged toward him. He gripped her around the throat and pinned her against the wall. She started fighting him, but he simply squeezed, shocking her into silence.

"Listen to me closely. This *is* a safe haven for women. No one is to force themselves on you. The men and women here freely explore each other. I have never forced myself onto a woman, and I never will. Ashley is mine. She's a fertile, which makes her life more valuable than yours. You think she'll be safe with my men here? Not all of them will be able to control themselves knowing there's a woman with a fertile future. I will never harm her. I will never force her. I'm the best chance she has in this world, and I will take her."

"Do you even hear yourself?" she asked.

He'd released her neck long enough for her to speak.

"I hear myself loud and clear. This world is a fucked-up mess, and I'm doing the best I can with what I've got, and believe me, take a look around you—it's not a lot. This is what we call home. Now stay, or fucking leave, but don't ever call me a rapist again." He threw her aside and walked back toward the library.

She clearly didn't understand how valuable Ashley was in the grand scheme of things. This was his world. His rules.

As he closed the library doors, the scent of musty old books filled the air, comforting him.

Ever since the virus had been released in the air, he'd only been surviving, moving from place to place until he found this mansion. Along the way he picked up a few strays, and they'd formed a sort of pack.

He took a seat in the worn leather armchair and stared out across the entire land of books. There were so many, and that was one of the reasons he loved this place. Of course, the security was tight.

The person who'd been here before had died. Their body had been in the hallway, and it looked like they were reaching out, trying to escape the death that wanted to claim them. He'd dug a grave and laid the body to rest far from the house before claiming the place. Washing every square inch of the building, he'd made it theirs.

Now there was a woman in his room.

A woman he wanted.

The sight of her alone had his dick hard. He couldn't recall a time he'd reacted this way to a woman.

Getting to his feet, he found the romance section and wondered if that would appeal to her sweet side. Picking up two romance books, he made his way back through the house, going toward his bedroom.

He entered his room and paused as he found her on the floor, curled up in a ball. She looked absolutely exhausted, and he saw the wet lines down her face from where she'd been crying.

Making her cry hadn't been his intention.

Locking the door, he put the books down on the small table and moved toward her. Compared to him she was incredibly small, fragile, vulnerable. Everything he loved in a woman.

He scooped her up in his arms and carried her over to his bed. She didn't wake, and he could only imagine the exhaustion she must be feeling. The world out there wasn't fit for most men, let alone women.

She'd come a long way, and he would do

everything in his power to win her trust. There's no way he'd ever allow another man to claim her, to touch her. She wouldn't feel fear.

Putting the blanket over her body, he teased back a few strands of hair. "You will always be taken care of. You have my vow on that, sweetheart."

He wasn't a bad man, not really. He only wanted her.

Pressing a kiss to her temple, he sat back and watched her sleep. If she had any nightmares, he'd chase them away. For now, his woman had to sleep soundly.

****

Ashley lost count of how long she'd been there. The days turned to nights, and nights turned to days. That first night, she'd gone to bed alone, but every single night since then, Draven had joined her. His arm banded around her waist, pulling her against him, demanding so much without a single word.

She felt the evidence of his erection constantly pressing against her back. He wanted her, and each night she expected him to rape her. Every time he came to the room, he always had a book with him. His demands were always the same. A kiss for the book or at least to read some of the book.

It surprised her every time he brought her food. She expected him to want some other form of payment for the pleasure to eat.

Standing at his window, she looked down at the grounds. She saw people, his people, milling around. Some were carrying firewood, and others were working the land. She'd noticed a small patch of earth that had been overturned where they were trying to grow fruit and vegetables.

There was a time she loved to have fresh strawberries dipped in rich, sweet cream.

"Morning," Draven said, entering his quarters.

She turned to him as he put the tray filled with food down. The two romance books he brought every single morning were still within his grasp. She had yet to read a single page.

Was it selfish of her to just want to sit and read without making any payment? Would it be so bad to give him what he wanted?

Glancing from the book to the owner, she averted her gaze as he watched her. She wrapped her fingers around the ink that claimed her fertile. Whenever he was in the room, it always made her nervous. The ink was what made him choose her, she was sure of it, and she hated it.

This ink didn't make her any different from Luanna or any other woman.

"Did you sleep well?" he asked.

"Yes."

"Good. I don't like you having nightmares."

Since sleeping in his bed, the nightmares had been chased away, but she didn't tell him that. The last thing she wanted was for him to believe he had some kind of power here.

"I should be downstairs helping everyone," she said, pointing out of the window.

"Everyone has a job to do, and you'd be bored."

She turned back to the window. "I'm a hard worker. I was before I got this stupid thing." She lifted her wrist to see. "I can be useful here. Please, I don't want to spend my entire life living in this room. I want to help. To do my part."

"You do enough."

Slamming her hand against the wall, she whirled around to look at him. "I'm doing nothing. You don't want me to do anything. Do you really think I'm happy with this? The only thing I'm good for is my fucking womb."

Rage filled her body. It took her by surprise, but it didn't stop her as she started to strip the clothes away until she stood before him naked. There was no point wearing a bra and panties. If all he wanted was her body, then fine. She would just have to give herself to the beast and hoped that once it was gone, she would survive it somehow.

"There. This is what you want, right? I'm right here, ready to do my duty." She stormed toward him. Grabbing the book from his hand, she threw it across the room.

Her hands shook, and tears filled her eyes. She wasn't ready for this. With her hands on her hips, she waited, daring him.

There was no point in being afraid, and all she could think to do was get this over with.

He stared up from her feet. His gaze went over every inch of her body until he landed on her face. He stood up, and she watched as he adjusted his cock.

Taking a deep breath, she forced herself to stand still. To stare into his eyes. For him to know that she wasn't going to be ignored.

The moment he was right in front of her, she was completely taken back by how big he actually was. He wasn't small by any means.

She flinched as he reached out to touch her. Clenching her teeth together, she waited for him to hurt her.

He tucked her hair behind her ear, and down he stroked until his finger was beneath her chin and he tilted her head back.

Keeping her eyes open, even as tears fell down her cheeks, she stared at him, waiting for the pain. A touch she never asked for.

He lowered his head, and still she didn't pull away. Her stubbornness stopped her from doing anything but staying still.

When his lips touched hers, she didn't respond.

Draven didn't rush. He explored her lips, taking his time, and against her own wishes, she started to find herself responding to his kiss. Wanting him. The hit of pleasure took her by surprise as her nipples started to harden.

Her stomach clenched, and she reached out, shocked by how strongly she felt this tug to touch him. He didn't move her to the bed. His finger stayed on her chin, keeping her head lifted even as she kissed him back.

This was the first ever kiss she'd been given.

Running her hands up his body, she wrapped them around his neck and moaned as she opened her mouth and he plundered inside her. It felt so amazing, so hard, and so everything she wanted.

Pressing her body against his, she gripped his shoulders, and still he didn't touch her. He didn't spread her legs and fuck her.

Instead, he pulled away.

She watched, amazed, as he licked his lips, and there was a glint in his eye. Something she couldn't read.

"I think for that kiss, you can read the entire book." He stepped away from her, and she saw the evidence of his arousal pressing against the front of his pants.

Why hadn't he taken her?

He picked up the book she'd thrown aside, and he put it on the tray.

Next, he picked up her clothes and knelt before her. He held her panties out, and seeing no reason to fight him, she stepped into the panties, and he slid them up her body, putting them into place.

She expected him to leave it at that, but he wouldn't. He helped her into her bra, trousers, and shirt. The socks she wore were the only things she'd not kicked off for him.

Once the shirt was in place, he held the bottom of the material between his fingers.

"I know you don't think highly of me right now. I'm being selfish with you, and I know that it scares you. I'm not going to hurt you, nor am I going to rush you. When you're ready, I'll take you. Show you what you want, and give you everything your heart desires. It's not safe for you to be with others."

Tears filled her eyes as he spoke. His voice was so soothing, so gentle. Hypnotizing.

"Why can't Luanna be here then?"

"She hasn't got this." He held her wrist up, his fingers stroking over the delicate ink.

"I hate this."

"I know. Something happens to men who see it. I don't know why or even how it happens, I just know it drives them crazy. They want what they can't have. My men are good people, and to make sure I don't have to kill them, and to keep you safe, it's why you're here."

"It's also why you've claimed me?"

"Yes, I *have* claimed you. You're mine, Ashley." He pressed a kiss to her cheek. "Thank you so much for kissing me."

He helped her into her seat and then walked out of the room.

She watched as he shut the door, and seconds later, he locked it.

This time, hearing the sound didn't fill her with a rage like it normally did. Maybe she really was safer on this side of the door. Ashley knew there was a bounty on her head, not to mention she was apparently a rare commodity to men.

Picking up the book, she stared at the cover. It looked like an old-fashioned historical romance. Running her fingers across the picture, she studied the man and woman in some elaborate pose. She giggled.

Would it really be so bad to give herself to Draven? To let him take her?

Her lips still tingled from the kiss, but he hadn't grabbed her, or thrown her to the bed and fucked her as any other man would try to do.

All Draven had done was explore her mouth. He'd been more than thorough. That kiss had been … everything.

Putting her fingers to her lips, she closed her eyes, thinking about how sweet, how beautiful that kiss had been.

It was her first real kiss. And she couldn't imagine any other man giving her a better experience.

When she'd been captured by the government, the doctors and nurses had all treated her like an object. Not a woman, not a person. Just a fertile thing to be used and exploited.

The ink sickened her.

She'd expected to feel that way about Draven's touch, but now, she wondered exactly how it *would* feel.

Chapter Four

There'd been talk.

No one dared say anything to his face, or make a move against him, but he knew. Draven always knew. If he wasn't at least one step ahead of everyone else, he wouldn't be where he was now. Weak men didn't survive in the new world.

A rogue group within his walls planned to make a play for Ashley. He'd heard the whispers, the rumors, and felt the tension. They'd sell her to the floundering government for the promised bounty. Maybe even fill her with their seed before handing her over.

The shed where they kept preserves had a stash of weapons being concealed in the back under heavy black tarps. They were planning something soon. He feigned being oblivious, but he'd be ready for them.

Over the past several weeks, he'd allowed Ashley more freedom around the complex. Daily walks, visits with Luanna in the gardens, and private time in the library. He always ensured he was close by, keeping a careful eye on her and everyone nearby. Now he had to rethink her liberties. Until he found out exactly who he could trust, she wasn't safe.

After all he'd done for the men and women under his care, if pissed him off that they'd turn on him for the promise of wealth. Greed, it seemed, was stronger than loyalty for some. When he discovered who'd been plotting against him, Draven would make an example, one that would never be forgotten. He'd make his message ruthlessly clear: mess with his woman, and die a slow, painful death. There could be no exceptions.

"Where's Ashley?"

The annoying friend ambushed him just inside the kitchen doors. He exhaled.

"She's in my room." He moved around her, preparing a tray of food to bring with him. Fresh grapes, slices of fresh cheese, crackers, and cherry pie.

"But it's two o'clock. She always spends time with me now," said Luanna.

He ground his teeth together. The only reason he tolerated this woman was for Ashley's sake. She grated on his nerves. If it were up to him, he'd have sent her packing weeks ago. "Not today."

She kept following him, trailing along like a bratty child. "Why not?"

"That's my concern. When things are safe, she'll be free to resume your daily visits."

"Safe?"

He'd said too much already. There was nothing to explain, and his information was sensitive. Draven wasn't sure who he could trust, but he hoped the traitors weren't any of his close men. He ignored her, filling his tray with things he knew Ashley loved. Her happiness did something to him, chipping away at all the hardened bitterness that had built up over the years.

"Did someone try to hurt her? Is she okay?"

He left the kitchen, heading to the stairs. When she wouldn't stop questioning him, he nodded to Luke, who'd been standing guard near the gates. He promptly escorted Luanna away, despite her protests.

Little natural light illuminated the stone stairwell. It was only the afternoon, but a storm was just on the horizon, blackening the sky, making it feel more like twilight. They'd been prepping for the monster storm all day, protecting the gardens, and securing everything that the wind could potentially damage. It wasn't far off now. He could smell it in the air, the promise of rain bringing back memories from the battlefields. Did he have any good memories left? The older he got, the more everything in his life blurred into one sick nightmare he wanted to forget.

He opened the heavy wooden door, the hinges creaking, and entered his room. The glass patio doors were open wide, the brisk breeze fluttering the white sheers.

"Ashley?" Draven set down the tray of food on one of the dressers and approached the Juliet balcony. Ashley leaned over the iron railing, staring off into the distance.

She turned when he touched her shoulder. "Sorry, I didn't hear you."

"It's a good storm." He nodded to the skies and heavy clouds rolling in. "We could lose power."

"Is that why I'm not allowed downstairs?" She looked up at him with those big blue eyes, full of innocence and trust. He could crush her so easily, but all he wanted to do was protect her.

"Partly." He strode back into the room, not wanting to lie to her, but also not ready to terrify her with the possibilities. He wanted to be her protector.

"Draven?" She kept up pace behind him. Even though his room was huge, he couldn't escape her. He stopped and turned, holding her shoulders.

"When you came here, you knew the world was a dangerous place for a woman like you. For a fertile."

"Until I came here. Until I found *you*."

He stifled a groan, briefly closing his eyes. She had no idea how much pleasure her words carried. He didn't want to let her down. And he wouldn't.

He'd been given a herculean challenge, one almost impossible to accomplish. But he'd managed to behave, even though his patience had been tested since her arrival.

Sleeping in the same bed. Listening to her giggle

as she'd read. The way she licked her lips when she played shy.

The curvy little virgin with the fertile band was driving him close to insanity. He swore she knew what affected him, how to make his cock hard with just a look. Her innocence was morphing, and her flirting was becoming incessant. The time for playing the gentleman was quickly growing old.

He'd already claimed her as his, and very soon he'd make that official. Fill her with his seed. Know every inch of her lush body.

"I won't let anyone hurt you," he said.

"No, something's wrong."

He shook his head. "I'm just being cautious. I've heard some talk, so I'd rather keep you with me for a while. The only person a man can trust is himself. I've learned that the hard way many times. Never again."

"What kind of talk?"

"Men planning to take what's mine."

Her mouth parted slightly. "I thought this was a safe haven."

"It is … or it will be once I find out who's plotting against me." He ran his hands from her shoulders, down her arms until he could interlock their fingers together. "They have no idea what they're up against."

"And if they win?"

He chuckled. "They can try to take you from me, but I'll never allow it. I won't be threatened by any man, Ashley. And I'm not afraid of getting my hands dirty."

Not only was he ready to take on any threat, he knew things about the group of traitors, and their next moves. He'd use the information to his advantage and slowly root them out. It wouldn't be long until he knew exactly who'd infected his perfect little world.

"I keep wondering why I'm still here. I mean, shouldn't I be afraid of you, too? Don't you want the same thing as other men? Money, power, legacy?"

"The government is broken, Ashley. It's struggling to gain any foothold in this shitfest, so it'll promise the world for a woman like you. You represent hope, a future—both things lacking in the world. They'll use you like a pawn." He took a breath. "Look around you. What good is money anymore? What can it buy? I don't need money or power ... legacy, that's something else."

She gasped when he stepped forward.

"Do you think men want me for money or for my body?"

"Both."

"Not you, though." She reached up and fiddled with the button at his collar. "You just like to have me around like some kind of collectible toy. I think you like having something that everyone else wants."

He smirked, unfastening a few buttons on his shirt. "You're intuitive."

Ashley shrugged.

"But don't mistake my obsession. I *do* want something more from you."

She dragged one finger along the bare skin where his shirt had parted. A crackle of thunder echoed in the distance. "Tell me what you want from me."

Draven groaned. "I want the legacy. You can give me that."

"So, you want my body."

"Yes, I fucking want your body, but unlike other men, I want the woman, too."

"Really?" She narrowed her eyes in disbelief. "There's nothing special about me beyond this band. I'm not unlike other women." She held up her wrist. He leaned over and kissed it, making her breath catch in her throat.

"You're wrong, little Ashley. You're very unlike other women. And I've been using more self-control the past many weeks than you can imagine."

"Why not just take what you want? You're the king of this castle, after all."

"You're right. I could have already filled you with my seed. My progeny would be growing inside your womb."

"You've barely touched me."

"I told you I can be a patient man. The world may be a cold place now, but I still hold out hope that one day you can love me."

****

Love?

She didn't expect a man like Draven to consider anything beyond power and desire. And she never expected to experience what she read about in the romance novels. It seemed the notion of love disappeared once survival took over people's basic values. It was a black and white world, void of color. There was no room for love and devotion when thoughts were focused on meeting their basic needs. The world was a scary place, and now Draven had changed everything with those few words.

Ashley realized she hadn't said a thing. Her thoughts were scattered, so many possibilities filling her head. Could she love Draven? Could she not?

For all her complaining, she savored being sheltered and coddled. It felt like a weight off her shoulders to be able to forget about foraging and safety, and enjoy the simple things. Draven made all that possible.

He'd made her fertility band a blessing rather

than a curse.

And she was tired of him holding back. How could a grown man sleep with her every night and keep so much self-control? She was starting to get a complex. Ashley had convinced herself he was using her for her womb, and one day he'd force himself on her. To hear talk of love and commitment tossed her expectations out the window.

Was he attracted to her? Or did her extra pounds turn him off?

Draven was hard and chiseled. She'd seen him working his body, the sweat glistening on his back as he did pull-ups in the archway every morning before he showered. Every day she spent with him made her more desperate for his attention. Yes, he talked to her, fed her, and spent time with her around the property, but she needed more.

She wanted him to look at her like a man full of hunger.

She wanted him to take without asking.

To claim her.

To fuck her.

You're such a freak, Ashley. You've been alone too long.

Luanna would be ashamed of her. Her friend refused to rely on a man and continually tried to convince her to leave the compound. Recently, Luanna had been pushing the idea more, saying they'd overstayed their welcome and it was no longer safe.

Ashley didn't listen because she didn't want to leave. What awaited her beyond the walls? Rape, starvation, harsh elements, and certain death before long. Why survive when they could live in Draven's kingdom? Being a fertile without protection meant she'd always have a target on her back, always be hunted by the worst of the worst looking to cash out or use her for their own sick pleasure.

"Have you ever loved a woman?" she finally asked.

He stared at her, his eyes turning black as the light was slowly snuffed from the room. The clouds blocked out the remnants of the sun, creating a foreboding atmosphere. All she could feel was lust.

"I never had time for it before the virus. After things changed, it never entered my mind. I've lived here, building and protecting, only focused on keeping out the worst and trying to hold onto the little humanity I had left."

"Love and survival aren't a very good mix," she said.

"No, you're wrong. These times put love to the test. It's finding it that's difficult."

She swallowed hard.

"With you, little one, I can see myself losing my head … and my heart." He cupped her cheek with one rough hand, and she instinctively closed her eyes and rested against this touch.

"I'm afraid to believe you."

"I could have taken everything from you, stripped you of your virginity without consent, or never opened my gates to you and your friend. But I've housed and cared for you for weeks in hopes you'd see my sincerity."

The last thing she wanted to do was push him away or appear ungrateful. He was right. Things could have gone so differently in other circumstances.

"I appreciate everything you've done for me. You have no idea. Before I came here, I'd lost all hope. Every day was a like a waking nightmare, and I kept praying the virus had been a figment of my imagination."

"You're appreciative." His words were clipped. "But you're not interested in a relationship with me."

"I never said that. Trust isn't something I've learned to hand over easily. And I may not have experience with men, but I'm here because I want to be."

He appeared to mull her words over in his mind. "You need more time."

She shook her head. "I need you to take control."

He wet his lips, and her stomach did a little flip. She'd seen how he behaved with the other people in the complex. He was strict and didn't put up with any bullshit. His softer side seemed reserved for her alone, and although she was grateful for the fact, she craved him to command her, to take her, to claim what he wanted.

"Like you've said, I'm the king. I'm always in control."

"Then tell me what you want. I'll do whatever you ask of me."

"Out of appreciation?"

"Because I want to be yours." It was hard to blurt out those words because she feared rejection from him. Feared everything. But for the past month, she'd been happy, and that was a lot more than she could say about her life before finding Draven.

"I like the sound of that." He walked around her. She stayed rooted in place. "I've never wanted anything more."

"Do you always get everything you want?"

"It seems so." Once directly behind her, he brushed her hair over one shoulder and kissed the back of her neck. The kiss sparked something inside her, something wanton and desperate. He knew exactly how to touch her, how to arouse her effortlessly.

His breath on her skin.

The scent of his cologne.

The heat of his presence.

She closed her eyes and let go, knowing she had to trust this man if anything was to develop between them. Without hope, what was the point of life? She had to believe something magical was possible.

More thunder boomed in the distance. Closer now. A flash of lightning briefly lit the inside of the darkened room, shadows flashing along the walls.

"Take off my shirt," he said, coming back to stand in front of her.

She undid the rest of the buttons, slowly, one by one. A dark trail of hair led lower into his pants. His abs were hard and cut, and she craved to run her nails along his skin. Instead, she pushed the material over his broad shoulders until it fluttered to the floor. There was a tattoo on his upper arm, and she let her fingers linger over the ink.

"Where did you get this?"

"In the Marines. Long time ago." He set his hand over hers, refusing to lose focus. The look in his eyes was what she wanted to see—hunger claiming his beast.

She removed her own shirt, leaving her in just her bra. The lacy cups barely contained her cleavage. Draven's jaw clenched as he stared. His need only made her hotter.

"I'll need you to teach me everything," she whispered. His restraint was admirable, but her body was screaming at her. She was ready for him, no more doubts and fears stopping her from moving forward. This was a risk she was willing to take.

"So you'll be a good girl for me? Do as you're told?"

God, that was exactly what she craved. The stress of survival, running for her life … it made her appreciate this little paradise. She wanted to let go and give Draven the reins.

"Yes."

He made a sound that reminded her of an animal, a savage beast ready to take down its prey. Draven peeled one cup of her bra down, her tit spilling out. The moment he covered her areola with his hot, wet mouth, she cried out. The intimacy and rush of heat took her off guard. His hands slid down to cup her ass, his fingers squeezing tight.

Draven feasted on her tits, peeling the second bra cup out of his way and alternating between both. He kissed his way up her neck, teasing the sensitive erogenous zones around her ear. She closed her eyes and savored all the new sensations. Ashley felt as if she was floating, her inhibitions sailing away.

"Such a sweet little virgin. All for me." He backed her up until she hit the dresser, then tugged her hair to one side, hard enough to make her squint. The evidence of his arousal pressed hard against her stomach. "Do you feel that?"

She nodded.

"I could have been with a lot of different women," he said. "But none of them did this to me. None of them made my cock hard and heavy."

"Are there other women?"

This new world was a mystery, a crazy place of injustice and lawlessness. She never knew what to expect. The last thing she wanted was to be another piece to a king's harem.

"I don't want any woman but you, Ashley. The day you walked through my gates, I knew it had to be you."

"Because of the fertility band?"

"Because of *you*."

His mouth came down over hers, a deep, sensual kiss that made her toes curl. She reached up and wrapped her arms around his neck, kissing him back with all the passion that had been growing inside her.

He reached down, his hand slipping into the front of her pants. She felt every movement, her body hypersensitive to his forbidden touch. He cupped her pussy, and she worried that he'd feel the wetness between her folds. Every touch, every kiss, made her pussy pulse stronger. Could he feel the heartbeat between her legs?

She dropped her weight a bit, and the feel of his bare hand against her pussy felt dirty and addictive. She wanted more.

"You're nice and wet for me. Your little virgin cunt is hungry for my cock."

Yes!

Any fears she had of losing her virginity were a thing of the past. She needed this man, this king, to make her a woman.

Chapter Five

The fertility band was getting on his last nerve. Draven saw how insecure Ashley felt, and yes, at the start, his need for her had started because of the band. What man wouldn't be turned on by the prospect of having a woman who was fertile? Who'd be able to take care of his children, to nurse them?

The virus had been sent out to destroy, and in the process, it had brought out the baser urges of the male sex. He wanted to mate her, to fill her with his seed and watch her body swell with his baby.

She let out a moan, and he loved hearing her sounds as he stroked her sweet pussy. Tonight, he didn't have to worry about any of his men attacking and trying to take his woman from him. With the storm about to rage, they had been sensible.

He liked storms. They always helped him to clear his mind, even when he was serving for his country. A storm for him always signified a change.

Teasing across Ashley's clit, he watched as her eyes closed and her mouth opened on a gasp. She wriggled against him, her nails sinking into the flesh of his shoulders as she held onto him.

"Do you have any idea what you're doing to me right now?" he asked.

"You're the one doing it to me."

He leaned in close and kissed her neck, right over her pulse. He wanted to do more than kiss.

Draven wanted to suck, kiss, to mark her so every man who saw her knew exactly who she belonged to. He wanted to drive his cock so deep inside her that she'd be dripping with his cum.

There was so much he wanted to do to her, and instead, he kissed her hard as he stroked her clit, but still it wasn't enough.

"I want to see your pussy," he said. "Do you trust me?"

She did that biting lip thing that he loved. "Yes."

"Good. I'm not going to take this any further until you want me, baby. I'm not going to rush you."

"I trust you."

There was an edge of need in her voice, and he loved the sound of it. He pulled his fingers from her pussy and tasted her. She was just as sweet as he imagined, and he couldn't wait to have her explode on his tongue.

She had nice, large tits, full and ripe, and ready to be taken.

He wanted to fuck her. His cock pressed painfully against the front of his pants, desperate to be inside her. To claim her.

As he pushed her shirt off her shoulders, he fingered the bra he'd been toying with. It was a little on the smaller side, but she hadn't complained. He'd been trying to find bras for her, but unless he ventured out of his castle, he couldn't get one for her size. She refused to go without one though and had even explained to him how hard it was for her to walk around without a bra. He didn't see a problem with her tits bouncing around. He loved seeing them, and often found himself watching her just in case she decided to give it a chance.

As he flicked the catch open, the bra fell, spilling her tits forward. He fingered one of the red lines caused by the bra.

"I don't like this. I don't like the thought of anything hurting you."

"It's fine."

He pressed a kiss to her shoulder, and he lifted her arm, seeing how red it was. Once he dealt with the traitors, he was going to plan a trip to the nearest town so that he could get her a bra that fit and didn't dig into her flesh.

"It doesn't hurt. Itches a little." Her cheeks were a flaming red, and he smiled.

"You don't have to be embarrassed with me."

"I'm not used to talking with someone like this. It feels too personal."

"I want you to talk to me about everything." He trailed his lips down her chest, going to her breast. Cupping the mounds, he pressed them together, staring at her rounded globes. His cock ached, but he slid his tongue across each peak, enjoying the pleasured sounds she made. She drove him wild, but he kept himself in check.

Licking one bud and then the other, he glanced up and saw the desire swirling in her eyes. She wanted this as much as he did.

After giving attention to both of her nipples, he let her tits go and slid his hand down her body to her pants. The jeans she wore were on the loose side, and as he flicked the button open, they fell to the floor easily.

He held her hand as she stepped out of them, kicking them to one side.

"I've never done this before," she said, repeating what he already knew.

Nerves clearly got the better of her.

"I'm not going to fuck you until you're ready." Even as his dick protested, he had to prove he wasn't only after sex. He wanted the whole package.

This was what made Ashley different from all of the other women. He didn't feel this protective need with anyone else. Ashley was the only one to inspire it within him. She made him feel human again, made him dream, and gave him respite from his survival mode.

With only her panties left, he gripped them and gently pulled them from her body.

She let out a little gasp.

"It's okay. I've got you."

"I don't know what it is you do to me. Sometimes I'm scared, but you make me feel so safe, cared for. It's like I can finally stop panicking about everything because I know I've got you. I'm sorry. I'm rambling on."

He smiled. "I think it's cute. You can talk to me all day long." He'd gladly listen to her, no matter what it was she had on her mind. He enjoyed her company.

She pressed her hand against his chest. "I want this."

"I've told you, no rush."

"It's not just about the rush. I don't know what it is, but I don't want this to stop." She slowly slid her hand down to his jeans. Her fingers were on the buttons. He waited, knowing what would come next. As she cupped his cock, it took every ounce of restraint not to pounce on her then and there.

Draven waited to see what she'd do next.

She opened the button on his jeans and slid her hand inside, holding him. He gritted his teeth.

"You're big."

"I know, but we're going to fit together. We're made for each other." He slowly stroked her arms, gliding the tips of his fingers up and down. She let him go and pushed his jeans down.

He let out a little hiss as the zipper of the jeans scratched him.

"Be careful there, sweetheart. I've got to take care of that guy."

"I'm sorry."

"You've got nothing to be sorry about." He

released his jeans and let her get her fill of him.

He didn't look away or try to cover himself.

Men came in all different sizes, and for him, he'd been blessed. Long and thick, and one glance down at his cock, he saw just how aroused he was with pre-cum leaking out of the tip.

She worked her hand up and down his length. Her touch was so light at first. "Does it hurt?"

"No. Never." If anything, his balls were killing him, but that was only because he wanted to empty them right into her tight cunt.

Control.

Don't fucking lose it.

He walked her back toward the bed, and as her legs hit the edge, he eased her down. The action stopped her from touching his cock, and for now, he enjoyed the sweet relief.

"I don't want to stop," she said, giving him that pretty pet lip.

"We're nowhere near close to stopping. I've got the whole evening planned." If she didn't want to go all the way, he knew there was more than one way to enjoy tonight. "Lie back."

She eased back, nice and slow.

He waited. He had all the patience in the world. At least, he liked to think he did. It was being tested when it came to Ashley.

"Spread those pretty thighs. I want to see what belongs to me." Just saying those words filled him with an overwhelming feeling of possessiveness.

All of his life, he'd wanted something for himself, and he finally had it in Ashley. The fertile woman who'd found him. She'd come to him for safety, and he was more than willing to grant it—for a price. Everything in this world had a bottom line.

For Draven, it was owning Ashley. Possessing her.

He wasn't going to allow those piece of shit traitors to take from him, not now, not ever.

She leaned back and lifted her legs, splaying them open as told. Her pussy was so slick, the fine hairs that covered her sex, soaked through.

"You like stroking my cock, beautiful?" he asked.

"Yes."

"What else?"

"I like it when you touch me."

She licked her lips, and he saw there was something else she wanted to say. He was curious.

"Out with it, pet," he said.

"I like it when you order me around."

He knew that already.

Draven stroked her pussy, lightly caressing over those wet curls. "You're going to need to get used to it because it's going to be happening an awful lot."

****

One touch from Draven was enough to set her one fire. Ashley wanted more than just his hand on her pussy. She craved his cock sliding inside her, filling her and sating that burning need.

Everything had changed since coming here to Draven's Kingdom.

Luanna constantly told her how nice he was, and compared to the outside world, this was heaven.

From the few times she'd been allowed outside, she saw the stares she got. Some of the women didn't like her being here with Draven. They were possessive of him, and she understood it.

The thought of him being with another woman filled her with so much anger and jealousy, both of which were completely foreign emotions for her.

Before being branded a fertile and having her whole life torn away from her, there hadn't been a man in her life. Not one person she could see herself spending the rest of her life with.

Draven was different. They had this connection.

Even now as she stared into his eyes, there was something about him that made her believe she was safe. Even as he wanted to fuck her, to take her hard, and to flood her with his seed, he wouldn't do it, not unless she was ready. It gave her a sense of power and peace.

She reached between her thighs and touched the lips of her pussy, spreading them open for him to touch.

Two fingers moved between her slit, teasing her clit. A rush of heat and energy made her body jolt.

"Are you sure this is what you want?"

"Yes. I'm yours, Draven. I'm ready."

Out there, in the wild, anyone could have her. Her life wouldn't be her own. She'd be passed around among men like nothing more than an incubator. With Draven, it was different. She wanted him as much as he wanted her. He aroused her, and above all else, he seemed to care.

She truly believed they could build a life together.

He moved his hand away, and she let out a whimper, not liking that he was making her wait like this.

"I'm going to make you beg, baby." He knelt on the floor between her thighs, and she moved to her elbows to watch him. Draven held her hips in place, and she cried out as his tongue started to tease over her clit. Just as she was getting aroused, he stopped. "You taste so good."

"Don't stop."

"You like what I'm doing to you?"

"Yes."

He chuckled, and she groaned. She'd never been

this needy in all of her life. She'd never wanted nor needed a man before. Any minute and she'd demand he fuck her.

Draven didn't keep her waiting. He sucked her clit into his mouth, his teeth biting down on the swollen nub, making her cry out and scream for more. He held her still as he attacked her pussy, more animal than man.

Each touch, lick, stroke, and suck took her higher and higher. She begged for more. She didn't want him to stop. She was completely at his mercy, his tongue creating a riot of wicked pleasure.

Not once did he push inside her or force her for more. He took his time, letting her get accustomed to his wicked touch. He made her burn and ache for more.

Holding her in place, she couldn't fight him off, not that she wanted to. Whatever he was doing with his tongue was too good to make him stop.

"You're going to come all over my mouth, and then I'll fuck you, Ashley."

She knew if she asked him to, he'd stop.

That was the point.

No other man would stop. Especially not anyone the government matched her with.

She gasped as he swirled his tongue around her clit before sliding it back and forth. This time, he didn't stop, and the magic kept on building, driving her higher and higher. His grip on her hips tightened to the point of almost being unbearable. There would be bruises tomorrow. She cried his name, and then he sent her hurtling toward the stars.

She'd never felt anything quite so magical in her life. The pleasure rushed over her entire body all at once, making her cry out, gasp, moan, and want so much more.

The feeling was so fleeting that at first, she couldn't believe it was over.

Draven pressed a kiss to her clit and moved up her body. He kissed her navel, then each of her tits, before taking her mouth. She didn't pull away, even as she tasted herself on his lips.

He slid his tongue inside, and she moaned, opening up for him to take even more.

"Tell me, Ashley," he said, stopping the kiss. "If you don't want this to continue, tell me to fucking stop."

She cupped the back of his hand and drew him down toward her, kissing him harder. "I want this." She spoke between kisses so he knew without a doubt what it was that she wanted.

Ashley couldn't think of a better way to lose her virginity than with Draven, right here, in this moment. She'd belong to the king, the one man all the women wished they could have.

His cock pressed against her pussy, not probing, but she knew it was there, ready to take her.

He reached down between them, and he cut off the kiss to hold his cock. He was so big and wide, and the tip was so wet already from his pre-cum.

She watched him place his cock between her sensitive, wet slit, and as he slid up within her, she gasped at the sudden hit of pleasure as he hit her sensitized clit. He thrust between her pussy lips, going up and down, and finally, he stood poised at her entrance.

His gaze was on hers.

Draven didn't slam inside her, claiming what was his. He waited. Giving her time to say no.

She was the one in control here. Not him.

Ashley didn't say a word. She waited.

Wanting this.

Needing it.

Waiting.

Finally, he pressed forward. He broke through her

virginity, and the sudden hit of pain took Ashley by surprise. She gripped his shoulders and released a whimper that she couldn't stop.

Draven slammed to the hilt within her, and she cried out. He was so big. He possessed every inch of her.

When he was seated deep inside, he stayed perfectly still.

"I can feel every single pulse and ripple, baby. You're so fucking tight. So tight." He kept on repeating the last part.

It was on the tip of her tongue to make him stop, to end this. She hadn't expected the pain and sudden nerves. But Ashley couldn't bring herself to do it.

She stayed silent, refusing to say a word. This had to get better. He'd already given her a taste of how good things could be.

Time passed. She didn't know how much, but she did hear the start of the wind howling outside, letting the world know it wasn't happy.

Right now, she felt just as unsettled.

Slowly, she started to wriggle. Draven kept on kissing her lips or her neck, sucking on her pulse, marking her flesh as his.

Sometimes as he moved, she felt the driving force of his cock, the one that had given her so much pain not long ago. Now her body was adjusting, and those wanton desires returned.

Ashley gasped as he slid in and out. It felt amazing. So full, so completely taken.

"Do that again."

"I don't want to hurt you."

"You're not. Please, Draven, for me."

He hesitated and then slowly slid out of her until only the tip was inside. She stared down at where they were joined. The smallest bit of blood coated his cock.

Her virgin blood.

Draven slammed in deep, and this time, she raised her hips to meet him. In and out, he thrust inside her, driving her pleasure higher and higher. His cock was rock hard, and he fit inside her so well. She didn't want him to stop.

"I'm not going to be able to last, baby."

She groaned.

Over and over, he drove inside her, pistoning like a machine. His muscles tensed under her touch. He plunged inside her one final time, and she felt his orgasm, each pulse of his cock as he filled her with his cum. It took her completely by surprise as the spray of his cum set off her own release. His pelvis against her clit provided the right kind of stimulus to give her a second orgasm.

He held himself over her until he finally collapsed. She didn't push him away but took his weight, more than happy to have him surround her.

"I wanted to make that last," he said.

Draven pushed up on his forearms, and she cupped his face. "That was perfect."

"I hurt you."

"You had to. I believe a woman's first time is always painful."

He lifted off her, and she bit her lip at the small bite of pain as he pulled his cock free. "I don't want to hurt you. Not ever."

He moved beside her, and she felt his cum starting to spill out of her pussy.

Draven touched her stomach. "I wonder if my baby is growing now."

Chapter Six

The storm howled between the cracks in the window panes, an eerie sound that woke him from his sleep. The dark room suffocated him, and it took him a minute to realize he wasn't in an army bunker but safe in his castle. Although "safe" wasn't what he'd use to describe his life right now.

He took a cleansing breath to calm his racing heart.

Draven wanted to enjoy his newfound happiness, to hold Ashley's warm body against his forever. But he knew trouble was brewing in his perfect little paradise. Weapons were slowly being taken from the storage lockers, and plans were coming into shape to overthrow his power. He felt it. And his instincts rarely led him astray. Every man and woman within the walls of his compound had been welcomed in. He offered safety, food, shelter, and as close to a normal life as possible in their twisted new world. Apparently, that wasn't enough for some of them. He began to regret being so generous.

Ashley stirred in her sleep. He stroked her hair, tucking her closer. The rhythmic rise and fall of her chest soothed him. He wanted to keep away all her nightmares, to give her the life she deserved. He would, despite the uprising in the works. He was on top for a reason, and he'd soon root out his enemies and make examples of them.

If Ashley became pregnant with his child, he needed to create a safe haven for a baby to grow up in. No way would he have his family living in fear.

His inner thoughts kept nagging him, so he quietly slipped from the bed, careful not to disturb his woman. He walked over to the window and rolled out his shoulders. Draven tugged the sheer curtains to one side, staring down at the courtyard. Despite the raging storm and late hour, he noted a flash of light low in the distance. It bobbed up and down until it disappeared behind a wall.

Normally someone carrying a flashlight wouldn't concern him. Things were different now. He tugged on his jeans and a rain jacket as he readied himself to investigate. Draven was careful not to wake Ashley.

He'd be back before she woke up.

The echo of the rain filled the stone stairwell as he descended. It was just after three in the morning, so unless there was some kind of emergency, everyone should be asleep.

He weaved around the obstacles in the courtyard—stacks of storage boxes, a wagon, and the water tower. Rain continually blurred his vision. He wiped his hand across his face as he tried to focus. There was little light, the moon hidden by heavy cloud cover.

"It's a little late to be up, no?"

The dark figure whirled around, rain dripping from her hair.

Luanna.

She froze, and he half expected her to try to bolt. Instead, she crossed her arms over her chest and stood her ground.

"What are your plans for us?" she asked.

He shrugged, narrowing his eyes. "Why are you up this late?"

"Something's not right."

Draven was cautious of his surroundings every second, always aware and ready for trouble. He'd become increasingly paranoid lately. "You shouldn't be out here at this hour. If you can't follow the rules, maybe this isn't the place for you."

"But you're okay keeping Ashley because she's a

fertile. That's not why I brought her here."

"Then why *did* you bring her here?"

Luanna paced, the rain making it difficult to hear her. "I don't know. Maybe so she didn't end up like me. I thought this place was a paradise. I tried to find it for the longest time."

"And now you're here. Lurking around in the middle of the night at exactly the same time traitors are stealing my weapons and planning to overthrow my reign. You know anything about that ... Luanna?"

"What are you talking about?"

Draven didn't answer. He just stared her down, trying to unravel her secrets. Could she be one of the conspirators? Things had only started going to shit after they arrived.

"Look, I don't know anything about weapons or overthrowing anything. I was just looking out for my friend. My only friend."

He took a breath. "She's asleep in my bed. Of her own accord. You brought her here to be safe, and I can guarantee it."

"When can I see her?"

There was no reason to humor this woman. He had what he wanted already. But Draven wasn't a monster. "After breakfast, I'll let you have a brief visit with her," he said. "In my room. I'm not risking her safety until I can ensure there's no threat."

"Fine. That's fair enough."

"Good, now how about you get some sleep."

She slipped away into the darkness, and he stayed rooted in place.

He looked around at the high walls, the heavy rain creating a mist that rose up from the courtyard. The damp coldness seeped into his bones, but he needed more answers. He pulled his handgun from the back of his pants and proceeded to the first weapons locker. As soon as he swung open the whiny iron door, deafening silence greeted him. He pulled on the light in the center of the room, the lone bulb swinging back and forth, creating a mix of shadows along the walls.

He strolled along in front of the rows of guns on the rack, doing a rough count.

"Boss?"

Draven looked up, but didn't raise his weapon. "What are you doing here, Luke? It's late to be up."

"My night on patrol," he said.

He hadn't even checked to see who was on watch. As much as he'd been focused on his own internal security issues, he had to remember the biggest threat was on the outside of the walls. They always had to be on guard.

But did he trust Luke? He'd been with him since the early days, but the other man also had nothing to lose. With his wife and child already dead, maybe he was involved with the plan against him. Maybe he was jealous of Draven's newfound happiness.

Or Draven was being overly suspicious of everyone.

"Anything interesting tonight?"

"That new girl was snooping around, but she does most nights. Have you decided if they'll be staying on with us permanently?"

Draven mulled the words in his head. His protective instincts briefly flared. "Ashley isn't going anywhere. Luanna's fate is left to be seen." He continued to walk along the wall of weapons. "Tell me, *Luke*, have you seen any unusual activity around the castle recently? Anything out of the ordinary?"

"No, nothing. Is there something going on I should know about?"

Draven chose his next words carefully because as much as he hoped Luke wasn't involved, he could be. He didn't want to raise any red flags. "Just a question." Draven winked.

"Well, so far no major damage from the storm," said Luke.

He nodded thoughtfully, then pulled the string on the lightbulb overhead, blanketing them in darkness. If Luke wanted to take him out, this would be the perfect chance for him to make a move. Draven was ready for anything. Craved it.

"You mentioned wanting to cultivate the east fields. It would be a good time with the ground so soft," said Luke. "I can get a group together in the morning."

Draven kept walking until outside of the weapons locker. He closed the heavy door behind him and locked up. "It's dangerous," he said. Tending to any of the fields outside of their protective walls was always a risk. Groups of rogue travelers often passed through and wouldn't think twice about killing any person in their path.

"It's always dangerous."

Was gathering together an excuse to exact their plan against him? His paranoia was growing wild. Why the sudden need to cultivate the fields? Why Luke?

"I know you're capable. If you think it's a good idea, you have my confidence," said Draven.

"It will yield a lot more food for the growing community. We should also consider expanding the walls."

"Of course. Have that arranged."

Just as he was about to return upstairs, there was a knock on the front gates. He rushed over with Luke, both with weapons drawn. After flicking on the floodlight, he saw two women and a teen boy standing outside, soaking wet.

"Who are you?" he asked.

"We're looking for shelter from the storm. Just for the night. We're heading west, looking for family," said the woman. As she adjusted her hood to see better, he noticed the marking on her wrist.

Another fertile.

He nodded to Luke, giving him permission to set them up for the night. They'd be under careful watch until they left in the morning. No one was to be trusted.

He walked back toward the staircase, feeling more unsettled than when he first woke up. He nearly tripped on something outside his bedroom door, the metallic sound breaking the silence. Draven squat down and picked up the heavy item in both hands. A crowbar. He palmed the cool metal, his mind wandering.

Draven rushed inside and went straight to the bed, pawing at the mounds in the comforter, finding them all empty.

"Ashley!" he shouted. "Ashley!"

He turned his head when a door creaked. Ashley stepped inside from the balcony. "Draven, where were you?"

"Sorry, baby. Did I wake you? Are you okay?"

"You weren't in the bed, and I got scared." A distant rumble in the sky punctuated her words.

"The storm's heading away from us now. Everything will be okay. Nothing to worry about." He approached her, realizing she was naked when he got close enough. The shadows highlighted her lush curves and also the fear in her eyes. "No need to be afraid."

He kept scanning the dim room, wondering who had tried to get in. Were they trying to kill him or steal his woman?

She rested her head on his chest, and he stroked

her hair. It felt right to have someone to be responsible for, someone to love, a person to make life worth living. He wondered how long it would take until she became ripe with his child. She was proven and marked as a fertile, and all his. Before long, she'd be pregnant. That's if everything was working with him. He began to wonder.

"Let's get back to bed," he said.

He stripped out of his clothes, and together they crawled back into their nest of blankets. Her little hand ran up his chest as she cuddled up close. "I heard the door close behind you. That's what woke me," she said. "The first thing that went to my head was wondering if you had another woman. Stupid I know."

Draven shook his head. "There will never be anyone else. I may not be a good man, but I'm loyal. Never doubt that, Ash."

She snickered.

"What is it?"

"I haven't heard that name since high school." Ashley sighed. "It seems like a lifetime ago."

"Do you like it? The nickname, I mean."

"I do ... especially the way *you* say it." Her fingers trailed higher until they lingered on his cheek. Her desire sparked in the air, and he couldn't resist. Draven leaned up on an elbow and kissed her in the quiet hush of his bedroom.

Just the two of them.

Just this moment.

Nothing else was a guarantee.

****

Ashley had very little anchoring her in this new, volatile world. Draven had quickly become her rock. He made her feel safe and loved, and any time away from him made her anxiety rise. She knew he'd protect her from anything.

She'd been worried after he left in the night, her imagination getting the better of her. Having him back, feeling his hot body close to hers, filled her with a unique peace and security. And her hunger for him was difficult to rein in. There was something about him—his rich scent, the hardness of his muscles, the mature scruff on his face, and the fact he was king. She couldn't pinpoint exactly what made him so irresistible, but she couldn't keep her hands to herself.

And she craved him again and again. She wanted to give him everything, to make him feel the same security she felt with him.

She didn't regret giving him her virginity.

Ashley wanted to give him the heir and family she knew he craved. Was it so wrong to want a happily ever after in such a twisted world? Was it selfish to want to raise a child in such uncertain times?

"Ash…" He kissed down her neck, her body sparking to life. Nothing seemed to matter when he touched her. He brought her out of reality to that perfect place where just the two of them existed. She closed her eyes, savoring the feel of his scruff against her skin. His soft touch made her skin break out in gooseflesh.

She parted her thighs without being asked, her pussy already wet and aching. Sex was such an easy escape, and Ashley could see how easy it would be to become addicted. "I need you," she said. Her voice sounded too loud in the silent room. Only the distant sound of the retreating storm broke the hush.

"I'll never say no to you, baby." He ran the backs of his fingers along her soft inner thigh, so close to where she needed him. She was already naked, and for the first time, she felt comfortable in her skin. Draven loved her big tits and every rounded curve. "Tell me what you want."

She licked her lips, her heart racing. "I want you to fill me with your seed."

He groaned, leaning over to kiss her mound.

Ashley gasped, squeezing the sheets in a fist.

"I'm going to give you all of this." He took her hand, wrapping her fingers around his big dick.

"It's so hard." She gave him a little squeeze, loving how easy it was to get a reaction from him. "And all mine."

"Can you take me again?"

Just then a siren wailed, loud and grating, like the ones she used to hear when the cities were being decimated. Draven bolted up and rushed to the window. Spotlights passed by the glass in slow circles.

"What's happening?" she asked, pulling the covers up to her chest as she sat up.

"There's trouble. Get dressed, and stay in the room. Understand?"

He rushed to get clothes on, and she was terrified he would get hurt or worse. She'd only just gotten him, and already couldn't imagine the rest of her life without him.

"What about you? It could be dangerous."

"I'll be fine. Don't open the door for anyone." Then he was gone.

Ashley knew how dangerous it was outside the kingdom. It was beyond survival of the fittest. Evil was widespread, and there was no room for decency left. It was so easy to forget living in Draven's Kingdom, but the sirens brought back bitter memories.

She got dressed, even putting on her shoes, just in case. It was torture being locked up in the tower, not knowing what was happening. She paced the room, moving from one window to the next. There was life below, men rushing about, weapons in hand. She couldn't make out what the voices were saying, so she tried to lift open the window.

That's when she heard noise from inside the room.

Ashley took soft steps, listening, her nerves frayed. Someone was trying to get in the bedroom door. Was it Draven? He had the key.

What would she do if someone broke in and wanted to hurt her? She had nothing to use as a weapon. Maybe she'd try to hide under the bed.

The door swung open before she could decide what to do next. She held her breath, not moving or speaking.

"Ashley?"

She exhaled. It was Luanna.

"I'm over here," she said, revealing herself in the dark room.

Her friend ran over, and they hugged each other. It had been a while since they'd been able to talk.

"How'd you open the door?"

"I didn't survive this long without learning a thing or two," said Luanna. "Are you okay? Has Draven hurt you?"

She shook her head. "I'm fine. Draven's been taking excellent care of me."

"I don't trust him."

"I love him," she said. As soon as the words left her lips, she realized they were the truth, right from her heart.

Luanna ran both hands through her damp hair. "There's no such thing as love. Not anymore."

She wouldn't argue with her friend, not after the life she'd led. It would be cruel to tell her how wonderful her life had transformed in the past months. Ashley believed she'd found her happily ever after with Draven.

"Luanna, you need to stop this. You wanted paradise? Well, you have it here. We both do. You'll never be happy if you see everyone as the enemy. This is our new beginning."

Her friend stayed quiet, and she knew Luanna was reflecting on her words.

"What's happening out there? Do you know?" Ashley asked.

"No clue. This place is going down. We should get out while we can, Ashley. Maybe we can find someone to remove your fertility band. I've heard rumors that some people salvaged some laser technology."

Her friend attempted to pull her along, but she fought back.

"What's wrong?"

"I'm not leaving, Luanna. This is my home now. I can't go."

She threw up her arms. "He's brainwashed you. Can't you see that? Any male will promise you the world because of that band. It means nothing."

Tears pricked her eyes. She refused to believe it. Draven was different.

"I could be pregnant already. I can't leave him. I *won't* leave him. If you were smart, you'd see this place for what it really is and give it a chance. The world outside these walls is a terrible place. You know that, Luanna!"

Luanna paced back and forth. Ashley noticed the figure in the doorway first.

"Luanna…"

Her friend turned, but it was too late. Three men plowed into the room, knocking Luanna to the ground. The first one grabbed Ashley by the arm and tossed her into another man's arms. He squeezed her so tight, she lost her breath.

"Get your hands off her!" Luanna shouted from the floor, and one of the men kicked her in the ribs.

Ashley screamed. "Don't hurt her!"

She dropped her weight, trying to get out of the man's grasp, but he was too strong. Ashley twisted and writhed, fighting with every ounce of strength. The man holding her reeked of body odor, making her stomach roil.

They dragged her towards the doorway, and she knew she had to fight being taken. The replay of her stint in the government facility came back to her. She refused to be an incubator, a toy for men to use and abuse.

"Let me go!" she chanted.

Luanna got to her feet and bolted to the balcony, swinging the doors open. She screamed for help, then turned and looked Ashley right in the eyes. "Oh God, the gates have been breached."

Cold dread made her shiver uncontrollably. This was a nightmare in the making. Her adrenaline rush must have given her added strength because a second man had to grab her ankles and they carried her through the room like a used carpet.

The man in the lead stopped dead.

A hulking frame blocked the doorway.

Draven.

Her nerves tingled as the relief cascaded through her veins. But he was one man against three, and there could be dozens more if the gates had been penetrated.

"You're touching my woman," said Draven, his voice eerily steady. "That was your first mistake." He grabbed the lead man by the shirt, tugging him under his arm long enough to break his neck. It happened so fast, so proficiently, that she almost missed it. The sickening sound was followed by the heavy body collapsing to the ground. Draven stepped over the dead man, evil dancing in his eyes. He moved forward without hesitation, without fear.

She'd never seen this side of him, but she knew he had a checkered past that continued to haunt him.

"Do you know who I am?" he asked. Draven held out both his arms to the side. "This is my kingdom, and I'm sure you've heard that I don't tolerate trespassers."

"We don't want trouble. Just the girl," said the man holding her legs.

Draven tutted, his stance dripping of a man with confidence. "Can't have that now, can I?"

Chapter Seven

Draven stared down at the cages in the basement. Ten men in total had been captured, five of his own men and five from the outside.

The small group with the fertile woman left at first light, probably glad to get away from his kingdom after the chaos last night. Draven couldn't provide the safe haven they probably expected, which pissed him off more.

Luke stood next to him, not saying a word. They had lost three more men because of Ashley. He knew there was fear growing within the camp. Running a hand down his face, he felt the night's stubble that had grown. He was so fucking tired, and his body ached.

The men were unconscious for the time being. Turning off the single light, Draven made his way up out of the basement, locking the door behind him.

Luanna sat at the kitchen table, holding a drink of honey and lemon. The lemons weren't fresh, but they'd salvaged those cheap-ass bottles from the supermarket. They had raided one a few weeks ago and gotten as much food and medical supplies as they could.

"You okay?"

"I'm fine."

"If you want to leave, you can. You're not taking Ashley with you."

"You still think this is safe? They were your men as well. How can you even think of keeping her here?" Luanna got to her feet, glaring at him.

"Have you been touched?"

"What?"

"It's a pretty simple fucking question. Have you been touched?"

"No."

"Raped?"

"No."

"Hit?"

"No."

"Abused in any way?" His voice grew louder as he demanded answers.

"No!" She screamed the last one.

"So you want to leave the safety of this house for the outside world? Luke, do me a favor, tell Luanna how often occurrences like last night happen?"

"That was the first one, sir."

"The *first* one. I run a tight ship here, Luanna. Tonight was a mistake on my part. I will never let it happen again. I'm sorry if you feel I'm not taking care of you or Ashley. I care about everyone's safety."

"If Ashley wanted to leave, would you let her go?" Luanna asked.

Draven paused. He didn't like that question or the way it made him feel.

Staring at her, he wondered if she had asked him that on purpose to make him feel so fucking crazy. There was no way he could let Ashley go, not now, not ever. The world was not what it used to be. Women couldn't just walk down the street, especially fertile women. Men would hurt her. They'd tear her apart for the need to breed her. She'd be nothing more than a vessel.

She'd never smile again or laugh.

She'd be completely broken.

The thought of her broken filled him with deep sorrow.

"You'd be signing her death slip," he said.

"But you'd let her go?"

"If Ashley couldn't stand to be with me, and I was one hundred percent sure that she wasn't pregnant with my child, I'd let her go." Was that the first lie he'd ever told? No, he'd been a master manipulator.

"She doesn't want to leave," Luanna said. "You have nothing to fear."

"What?"

"I wanted to leave last night when I realized how dangerous it was. I feel responsible for her. She helped me when she didn't have to. That stupid fucking band, it'll get her killed."

"Not while she remains in my protection."

Luanna snorted. "Your protection. Your own men wanted her."

"That is not going to happen again," Luke said. "Most are loyal to him. He's helped us all to survive. Those men down there, they are ungrateful for the life Draven has given them. We have a chance here. Out there, you're nothing."

He saw the tears in Luanna's eyes. Draven grabbed Luke's shoulder. "Thank you."

"I would never choose out there, Draven. I'm loyal to you and you alone. One day, I hope one of the women would ... grant me their hand and allow me to make a good husband to them. I have no desire to go out there to be killed. I will die here, protecting our lands and our future." Luke nodded at him, then at Luanna before moving away, leaving them alone.

Luanna dropped back into her seat. She let out a little cough and took a drink of the lemon and honey.

"You're sick."

"I've been checking out the perimeter at night. A couple of nights ago, I fell asleep outside. Woke up soaking wet and cold. It's my own fault."

"Why do you not trust me?" Draven asked, staring at her.

"I don't trust any men."

"You're going to have to learn to trust the men

here, Luanna. We won't hurt you."

She took a sip of the drink. It smelled disgusting, but then he didn't like lemon, hated the taste.

"Do you think it's ever possible for the world to go back to the way it was before all of this?" she asked.

He shrugged. "No."

"You don't even have hope?" she asked.

He ran fingers through his hair. Ashley cared about this woman, even though from what he knew, they had only actually met each other days before coming here. How could two women have a bond that close already? He didn't get it. Still, to keep Ashley happy, he needed to try to … build bridges with this woman. To maybe have a friendship with her and that way, it would help Ashley feel more comforted by him.

"It's good to have hope, so I can't tell you to not have it. It'll be good for all of us to have someone around here forever hopeful that the future will be a lot better than the past we've all experienced."

"You don't believe in hope?"

"All the shit I've seen, I don't have hope, no. What I have is a desire to survive. I don't want to die. I know many of you want things to go back to the way they were, and maybe if we continue to build this fort, or this paradise, we can find some semblance of that past here. The world has changed. Even if it was to go back, there has been too much death and murder. Could you live next to a man who killed and raped a woman who wasn't fertile? Or butchered men for his chance at a woman?"

She bowed her head, looking into her drink.

"You want to take Ashley out into that?"

"I want us to be safe."

"You're safe here," he said. "All you've got to do is pull your weight, do the chores that are required, and you can stay here for life. Once I've dealt with those pieces of shit, Ashley will be able to walk around freely. Or at least as much as possible."

She looked up then. "You do care about her?"

"Of course."

"It's not just about her being fertile?" she asked.

He was starting to get irritated by everyone assuming he wanted her for her body and womb. "It's not just about her being fertile. I know it's crazy, but she's different than anyone I've ever known. There's an innocence around her that I want to protect at all costs. We need people like her." Draven took a breath. "She's not the first fertile to come through these gates. My desire for her has nothing to do with the band, and everything to do with *her*."

"You sound in love." She sipped at her drink, smirking.

"I've got to go and check on the perimeter. Try not to do anything rash." He turned away and left the large mansion. He didn't look back, nor did he look up to the top window to see if Ashley was watching him. He'd found some more romance books stored away in the library and he'd taken them to her. She'd been sleeping, and he made sure not to wake her.

It was hard to leave her. He loved watching her sleep. More often than not there was a sweet smile on her lips that tugged at his heart. He never wanted her to lose that ability to smile, to laugh. This world was shit, but not all parts of it had to be.

His first stop was the main gate. He checked the locks and bolts were firmly in place. He checked the electric box off to the left and saw everything was up and running again. No one was getting in or out without his say-so. He controlled the gates. Moving past the electric box, he walked along the main wall, checking for potential security issues. Bricks could easily be smashed in, and he demanded a full inventory of each section of wall during the day and night to make sure there were no weak spots. The perimeter took him close to three hours to walk. He wanted to do a thorough job, until he was satisfied with their security. Making his way inside the house, he went straight to the roof. He held a pair of binoculars and checked past the wall. He couldn't see too far, but he liked to check if there was anything odd like campfires or something out of the ordinary.

"Sir," Luke said, interrupting his thoughts.

"What is it?"

"The traitors filled our pantry with rats. Some of the bagged containers of rice, pasta, and grains have been destroyed."

Draven cursed.

They had gotten a good couple of years' worth of supplies built up. His anger grew, and all he wanted to do was slaughter those sons of bitches down in the basement.

"We're going to have to venture out beyond the gate," he said. "I'll come and check what supplies we have now, and we'll make arrangements as to how long we've got. If we have more people arrive, we may have to turn them away."

"I know, sir. We all trust your judgment."

He was pleased someone did. Right now, he was ready to paint the basement walls red and he'd not even seen the damage.

This had turned into one bad day. He needed a break.

No, he needed inside his sweet woman, that's what he needed. Following Luke off the roof, he made his way down to the storage area. He passed several of his people on the way, and they all looked nervous.

Before he even saw the mess, he knew it was going to be bad.

****

Ashley wondered when he'd come to see her. It felt like an eternity since she last saw Draven. She hadn't even seen Luanna either. Everything had happened so fast.

The secrecy and being locked in a cage were starting to wear thin. It may not be a literal cage, but she was a full-grown woman who could make her own choices. She was tired of being trapped in this bedroom. Why couldn't she be out there with everyone, helping?

She placed a hand on her stomach and nibbled her bottom lip.

"What do I do?"

She had no idea what this situation called for. Draven wasn't hurt. She'd watched him walk across the gate. Her vision hadn't been perfect, but she'd recognize him anywhere. Running her fingers through the strands of her hair, she stared out. The sun had gone down, the moon filling the night sky, and the rain had started again. She loved to see the trails as it ran down the window.

"It's going to be fine," she said.

Her legs started to get numb from sitting in the same position for so long. Getting to her feet, she swung her hands out, trying to get some circulation going. Stretching down to her toes, she lifted her hands above her head.

Her thoughts drifted back to the hospital where she'd been kept. Staring at the band on her hand, she still hated it as much now as she did then. The brand of ownership. She'd become the government's possession, not her own. It was so unjust.

The sound of the door being unlocked pulled her from her thoughts. Once she saw Draven, she didn't even allow herself to hold back. Throwing herself into his arms, she wrapped her legs around him.

"Thank God, I was so worried. I didn't want anything to happen to you." She slammed her lips down on his.

Draven held her ass, keeping her steady as he kissed her back. She missed his lips and his touch.

She sensed a sadness in him, and it made her pull away with a frown. The seriousness in his eyes made her aware of something bad about to happen. Her unease grew when he kept quiet.

"What's going on?" she asked. "Don't even say it's nothing." She knew he tried to protect her as much as possible. She wasn't a child.

"It's … I've got to organize a party to go and get supplies."

"Supplies? I thought you had enough food," she said.

"I did. During the attacks, they didn't fucking think ahead, and the pantry was filled with rats. They're all gone now, but they've ruined our supplies. There's not enough to feed us all for a week."

"That's bad, right?"

"It is. There's a chance I've got to leave for a few days. I won't take any cars. I don't want to risk drawing attention to us. After last night's attack, I don't want to leave the compound, but I've got no choice."

"Can't you send other people out?" she asked.

"I could, but I know my way. I know what I'm looking for. I'm military. I know what I'm facing. Half of these men have the minimum training needed to come back with adequate supplies."

She felt tears spring to her eyes.

"No, you can't go." She touched his chest.

He covered her hand. "I've got to."

She shook her head. "It's dangerous out there."

"You're worried about my safety?"

"Of course, I am. I don't want anything to happen to you. I care about you." She cupped his face and couldn't resist kissing him again. "Please, Draven, don't go."

He moved her back toward the bed. He'd already let her go, and she followed his lead, stepping back until the bed hit the backs of her leg. Draven didn't stop there, and she fell back to the bed.

Heat filled her body. She wanted him so much. His strength. His dominance.

Cupping the back of his neck, she kissed him with passion, getting lost in his taste.

"You drive me crazy," he said. His hand rested on her hip, and the evidence of his arousal pressed against her core. Just imagining him naked and inside her made a thrill rush through her body.

"You want me," she said.

"Yes."

"Then take me, Draven. I'm yours. Only yours."

"You know what to say to make it impossible to resist you." His lips trailed down her neck, and as he sucked on her pulse, she gasped, closing her eyes.

"I believe in fasting," she said, trying to contain her moan at his kisses.

He laughed. "We'll all starve. I've got to go, but tonight, I'm all yours."

"All mine?"

"Yes." He kissed her again.

Suddenly remembering Luanna, she pulled away from the kiss. "What about Luanna?" she asked.

He groaned. "What about her?"

"Is she okay? Is she safe?"

"What is it with you two? You've not known

each other that long."

"We helped each other. In this world you've got to take your friendships seriously or you'll lose them. I've already lost so much. I don't want anything to happen to her. I know she wants to leave. She hasn't left, has she?" She didn't want to leave Draven, and she couldn't think of anywhere else that could be better than here.

Luanna was safe here, Draven made sure of it.

"No, she's not gone. I spoke to her earlier today. I don't know if she's going to remain here. She wants to see you."

"Will I be able to see her?"

He paused, and she hated the hesitation.

"I'm not going to leave," she said, trying to coax him to agreeing to seeing her friend.

Draven sighed. "Fine. I'll allow it tomorrow, but you're not allowed to leave this room. There's only so much stress that I can take. I'll make sure men I trust are here as well."

"No, no. You've got to take men with you so I know you're safe."

"Ashley, you're going to be the death of me."

She chuckled. "I know." She kissed him again. "I don't want Luanna to ever leave."

"There's not a lot I can do about that. If she wants to go, I can't force her to remain."

She pouted.

"Don't give me that face, Ashley. I'm doing the best I can." He rolled off her, staring up at the ceiling.

Seeing the stress in his eyes, she was hit by a wave of guilt. She straddled his waist, running her hands up his chest and back down again. His cock was still hard. "I'm sorry. I'm asking too much."

"You're not asking too much." His hands

dropped to her thighs, holding her. She loved his touch. His hands were so warm and strong. "I just don't like it when I can't give you what you're asking for."

She waited as he stroked her thighs. She stayed still, not knowing how to initiate sex. Was it what she wanted?

"What are you thinking right now?" he asked.

"I ... I'm wondering what you're thinking."

"You're lying to me."

"I'm not." Her cheeks started to heat at the blatant lie.

He spun her around so that she was back on the bed and he was the one above her. "No?"

She pressed her lips together, trying to suppress a laugh.

"So you're not thinking about how best to get me into bed?"

"No."

"You're lying."

"I don't care if it's on a bed or not." She gasped, slapping her hands over her mouth.

He chuckled. "Now that is a sexy thought. I can fuck you on the floor, on your knees, up against the wall, in the shower. I can take you wherever I want." His lips began to work down her body, going to the tips of her breasts.

Gritting her teeth, she tried not to make a sound, not wanting him to stop. Her nipples were so hard from arousal. It would be so easy to give into him.

I want to give into him.

When he took one of her nipples into his mouth, she cried out. The pleasure went straight to her clit, sparking a need so great she began to rock up against him, needing friction between her thighs.

"Do you know what you need?"

"I need you. Please," she said. There was no way she was going to hide from him. The lust flooding her body was because of him, and she wanted sex.

There was no point denying her attraction, not for a single second.

"I love seeing you like this. You're so needy. It makes my cock ache. All I want to do is fill your cunt with my seed, pump it into you until you breed for me."

"Yes."

"You like it when I talk dirty?"

"Yes." She grew frustrated. Taking hold of his hand, she placed it between her thighs, letting him know where she wanted his touch.

He could talk all night so long as he helped her with her release. He rubbed her through her clothing, and there was too much in the way. She pulled on his shirt, trying to take it off him, not wanting him to be dressed.

Skin on skin.

Touch.

Draven.

She wanted only him.

He seemed to know what she wanted as he helped her to rid them both of their clothing. Within a matter of seconds, they were back on the bed, and she ran her hands over his erection. His heavy cock pressed against her pussy but not inside her.

"How wet are you for me?" he asked, his hand skimming the inside of her thigh. He didn't touch her where she needed him. No, he stroked over her pussy but not quite touching her.

She whimpered.

"Beg me, Ashley."

"Please, Draven, please, I need you."

"Who do you belong to?" he asked.

She stared into his eyes. "You. I'm yours. Are

you mine?" She hated how insecure she felt in asking the question.

He kissed the tip of her nose. "You have me."

Chapter Eight

Ashley didn't want him to leave, and he didn't want to leave her. Draven had no choice. Life was about survival, and without food, they wouldn't last long. The peace in his community was in part due to meeting everyone's needs. Once they got hungry, their ugly sides would emerge as they fought for every last scrap.

Draven wouldn't let that happen, not after all the work he'd put into his kingdom. Not with Ashley possibly pregnant with his child. He had a lot to live for now.

They took the old wooden cart and two horses. It kept them off the radar more than traveling with a truck. Scavengers went crazy for gasoline or working vehicles. He'd decided just to take Luke. Two men wouldn't rouse as much attention, plus he wanted as many bodies as possible protecting Ashley and his people.

"You love her," said Luke. The clickety-clack of the wooden wheels over the stony ground had lulled him the past hour. Draven was deep in thought, thinking to the past, and dreaming of the future.

"You can tell?"

Luke chuckled as he held the reins of the horses. "It's written all over you. Some say you're using her for her fertility, but I know better."

"Because you were in love."

He nodded. "That seems like a lifetime ago. It's time for me to start over, too."

"That's a healthy way to think. You're still young. No sense spending the rest of your life alone."

"I remember, not so long ago, when you preached relationships were a waste of time."

Draven smirked. "That was before Ashley showed up."

"What is it about her? God knows you could have had your pick over the years. I see how women swoon over you."

Draven couldn't really pinpoint it himself. "Maybe chemistry? Fate? I'm not sure why I fell in love with her, but it happened hard and fast."

"It helps that she's marked. You can have a family together."

His hackles rose. Lately he'd been thinking more about Ashley having a baby. What if he was infertile? The virus had affected some males the same way. If he couldn't have children, maybe she wouldn't want anything to do with him. The possibility had been putting him on edge lately. He couldn't lose Ashley.

"Yeah."

"Oh, that's not good," said Luke.

"Just another obstacle."

A forest was fast approaching. They'd have to go around with the wagon, adding more time to their trip. He only had a vague recollection of this route, but he knew it was the direction to the food storage facilities he'd used in recent months. Nothing was a guarantee, but it was the best lead he had.

"Once we plant the new fields, we won't be so reliant on outside food sources," said Luke.

"That's the idea," he said.

Draven wasn't worried about the extra time going around the forest. Natural barriers were perfect ambush sites. Although they had weapons in the back of the wagon, it was impossible to know what they'd be up against. It was foolish to expect this food run to be uneventful. They always had to prepare for the worst.

"Horses are getting antsy." Luke had to shorten the length of the reins.

"Go wide." Draven reached for the binoculars

and scanned the gaps between the trees, looking for any movement.

He wasn't worried for himself. Or Luke. For the first time in his life, he had a fear greater than death. He wanted to return to Ashley, because nobody could take care of her like he could. If he never returned, God knows what would become of her or his kingdom.

"Anything?"

"No." Draven lowered the binoculars. "Hopefully it's nothing."

When they drew close to the forest, they stayed to the far right. Only the sound of the horses snorting and wagon wheels struggling over the uneven terrain could be heard. He was on edge, not daring to say a word as he stayed focused.

It felt like hours passed as they slowly crawled by the sprawling forest. The town he wanted to reach wasn't far beyond these woods. It seemed to be going well when Luke noted something ahead. A natural barrier, maybe downed trees from the storm they'd just had. Draven saw a lot of damage during the ride, and one of the rivers was overflowing its banks.

"Whoa." Luke brought the horses and wagon to a stop.

"I don't like it. Doesn't look like storm damage to me."

Luke shook his head. "Looks like a fucking beaver dam, but I don't see any water."

His senses were firing off hot. Someone wanted to box them in, but so far, no signs of anyone.

"Maybe it's abandoned. We haven't traveled this way in over six months." Draven had to keep positive. The roadblock couldn't be monitored every minute of the day.

"Hands up." A man shrugged off the carpet of

grass he'd been hiding under. Several others followed suit. They all pointed weapons at them.

"We're just traveling through. We don't want any trouble," said Draven.

"What do you have in the wagon?"

"Nothing. We're just looking around for food and supplies, like everyone else."

The big guy came closer. He didn't look like he'd showered or brushed his teeth in years. "You must be coming from somewhere. There a settlement around here?"

He shook his head. Draven's heart raced. He'd never give up his kingdom. He hoped Luke didn't rat them out.

There were four men and only two of them, not to mention their weapons were stored in the wagon and out of reach. The ambush came fast and unexpected, not giving him a moment to react.

"Just kill them," said one of the men. "Less trouble down the road. There's only so much supplies to go around."

The leader aimed at Draven.

So many memories came flooding to mind. The days he'd nearly died in the war. Surviving this crazy new world. The future with Ashley he'd never know.

"Lower the gun. Nice and slow, asshole."

Draven turned around. It was Luanna, standing in the wagon with one of his automatic weapons in hand. Ashley was behind her, aiming a shotgun at the other men.

The men complied, dropping their guns to the grass. Draven and Luke immediately hopped out of the wagon and collected the guns, and patted down the foursome to be safe.

When everything had been secured, he walked to

the wagon and looked up at the two women. "Is someone going to tell me what the hell is going on?"

"Well, Ashley didn't want you going without her, and since I know a lot of good places for food and medical supplies, I thought I could be an asset," said Luanna.

"And you've been hiding in the wagon all this time?"

Luanna shrugged. "We were waiting until you got to town so you couldn't send us home."

"I wanted you safe, Ashley."

She set the shotgun down and reached for him. He helped her down, swinging her around in his arms. "I'm glad I didn't listen, or you could have been killed."

"I'm sure I would have found a way out of this mess. I always do," said Draven.

"You sure are smug, aren't you?" said Luanna. "A simple thank you would have sufficed."

"Thank you. I still don't approve of Ashley being at risk," he said.

"Well, we're here now," said Ashley, looking up at him with those gorgeous blue eyes. "Let's get the mission done and get home."

"What about them?" asked Luke.

The part of him holding onto his humanity demanded he show mercy. But it was a small part. The rest of him knew these bastards wouldn't stop until they found their compound, and they'd try to kill them on their return trip.

"Why don't you and Luanna handle this? We'll keep heading around this damn road block. I'm sure you'll be able to catch up on foot." Draven kissed Ashley and helped her up into the front of the wagon. He climbed up beside her, this time with a weapon near his foot.

He didn't want Ashley to think he was a monster, but he also knew Luanna was almost as ruthless as he was. She'd never allow the men to go free with their lives.

These were difficult times, and survival of the fittest had become a way of life. Those men were going to kill them for no reason except they were breathing. Nothing could be more ruthless than that.

****

Ashley scanned the area as they rolled along. The town was desolate, like a ghost town from old television shows. There was even tumbleweed crossing their path. As she'd recently learned, it wasn't a sign of safety. Man had become their biggest threat. It was ridiculous when food, shelter, and survival should be number one on everyone's mind. People turned evil way too easily. It was disheartening.

"It's too quiet," said Luanna. She stood behind them with a rifle in hand.

"It's deserted. Just be on alert. We'll get what we need and get the hell out," said Luke.

Draven squeezed Ashley's knee, offering her a bit of comfort. She wasn't used to this. Life in the kingdom had spoiled her, giving her a sense of false security. If only it was real.

"Do you think there will still be food here?" Ashley asked.

Draven nodded, giving her a little smile. She was so lucky to have found him. Ever since the virus, her life had been turned upside down. He alone managed to give her balance.

"Over there," said Luanna.

They stopped the wagon, and everyone got out. "Stay close to me," said Draven. They all had weapons, sweeping the area as they moved in on the store. If they could find the stockpile of food, Draven would have no reason to leave the kingdom. They could be safe and focus on living life and loving each other.

She placed her hand over her lower stomach as they walked, wondering if she was growing a child at this moment. More than ever, it was essential they find what they were looking for.

Luke kicked open the back door in the store, Draven moved in and did a sweep.

"All clear."

When they entered, the defeated look on his face told her everything. The room was ransacked, empty boxes and spilled bags of food strewn across the floor.

"Oh God," Luanna whispered.

She held onto Draven, holding back tears. Ashley needed to be strong and not make Draven feel worse. "We can start the planting, prepare new fields," she said.

"We need food now, baby, not next season."

They left the room, dragging their feet.

"Let's split up. There could be a few things left to scavenge," said Luanna. "I'll go with Luke and head east."

"We'll go west. Meet back at the wagon in twenty minutes. Fire a shot if there's trouble," Draven said.

They held hands as they walked up the sidewalk. It was surreal, everything frozen in time. Most of the people died from the virus. Of the remaining women, most were left infertile. Her thoughts scattered in so many directions. She wondered what became of the people who lived here. A tricycle lay in the dirt by the sidewalk, an eerie reminder of what used to be.

"If it wasn't for the virus, I never would have met you," she said. "I must be a monster for not wishing I could turn back time and ensure it was never unleashed."

"You're not a monster."

"Can I tell you something?"

He stopped, leaning against the wall of a hardware store. Draven holstered his gun and held her waist. "What is it?"

She swallowed hard, determined not to cry. "This all feels like a nightmare I want to wake up from. The death, the shortages, the hate. It's killing me from the inside out. Those books I read at home aren't just entertainment, they're my only escape."

Draven cupped her face, and his eyes appeared glassy. "Tell me what to do. I'll do anything for you, Ashley."

"I just want to pretend. Even for one day. To forget everything and feel like a normal man and woman in love."

Even in the kingdom, he was constantly protecting her and restricting her movements. She knew he was trying to keep her safe, scared to lose her. But it would be so nice to close her eyes and pretend there was nothing to hide from.

He glanced up and down the street, then opened the door to the hardware store. "We have twenty minutes, sweetheart. Time to start pretending."

Draven hoisted her up on the low check-out counter, then tugged off his t-shirt. Her body immediately reacted as she raked her eyes over his hard-muscled frame.

"Are you sure about this?"

"You're not the only one who needs an escape. I thought I'd never see you again when those men had us at gunpoint. I've never felt so desperate before. I have something to live for now, and I don't want to lose that."

She ran her fingers along the stubble on his cheek. "I love you," she said.

"You're my everything." He lifted her shift off and unclasped her bra. "There's a lingerie store in town. We'll stop by before we leave, get everything you need."

Her tits felt heavy, her nipples aching for stimulation.

Draven leaned over and suckled her breast. She closed her eyes and groaned. Ashley needed a release in the worst way. All the fear, tension, and stress had turned purely sexual.

"I love these tits." He sandwiched his face between them. "Fucking perfect."

He made all her insecurities disappear, made her feel like a queen.

"I need you," she said.

They kissed, hard and desperate. His tongue was teasing, tasting. Nothing else mattered except them and the bubble of time and space they occupied.

He helped her wiggle out of her pants from her perch on the counter. When she was naked on the cool laminate, he spread her legs wide. Her body began to heat from the inside out. She felt so exposed, even if it was a store in a ghost town.

"It's just you and me, baby. Nothing else matters right now." He squatted down, then lapped at her folds. She dropped back to her elbows, savoring his wicked mouth on her pussy. God, she needed this, needed Draven. He was born to give her pleasure.

He suckled her clit, slow and methodical, driving her crazy. The pressure in her cunt grew by the second, higher and higher, until he had to hold her thighs to keep her from squirming.

Right when she began to see stars, he pulled away, leaving her breathless.

"More," she whimpered. Didn't he realize how close she was?

Of course, he did.

"I want you to come around my cock, hot and tight, milking every last seed from me."

She panted, reaching for him. He only tutted as he unbuckled and pulled down his zipper. His erection was thick and huge, bobbing once he released it. Ashley watched with rapt fascination.

"Is it all mine?" she asked.

"All yours. I'm only for you." He smirked. "And this?" Draven impaled her with two fingers, hitting her G-spot in just the right way. He finger-fucked her until her eyes lolled back in her head.

"Yours!"

His cock replaced his fingers, filling her so full of meat that she gasped and begged for it all. He fucked her on the counter, holding her hips to keep her stable. Only the wet slapping sounds of sex could be heard in the abandoned store. Draven was a machine, taking away all her thoughts and worries. Some things fell off the counter, scattering on the tiles. Nothing mattered.

"You like it, baby? You like my cock deep inside you?"

"Yes."

"I'm going to keep fucking you until you're ripe with my baby." He pulled almost all the way out, then slammed back in. Every time he filled her, his pubic bone rubbed her clit. She was so close to coming all over his cock.

"Breed me," she chanted. Ashley knew he loved the words. Being bred by her king aroused her effortlessly. He wasn't being forced on her. She wanted him, wanted his love forever.

She combed her hands into his hair, now nearly down to his shoulders. They kissed as they fucked, making love, forgetting the world.

"Come for me, Ash."

She was so close, balancing on a precipice. It only took a few more hard thrusts for her orgasm to burst forth, her entire body jolting as she pulsed around him, forcing him to come inside her. She felt it all, his thick release, his fingers digging deep into her flesh as he came.

They slowed down, the beautiful release still surrounding her. She never wanted this time to end, never wanted to return to reality.

"I like pretending with you." He gave her a kiss and picked up her pants. "We should do it more often."

"Now we have to go back to reality and the fact we have no food," she said.

He kept quiet, pulling on his shirt and grabbing his gun.

The sunlight warmed her skin once they were back outside. It felt good after days of rain and cloud cover. They returned to the wagon. She saw Luanna and Luke waiting.

"Any luck?" asked Luke.

"We still need to check the warehouse I came to see," said Draven. "Get the horses ready."

She sat up front with Draven again. Ashley noticed that Luanna and Luke were getting very friendly. She pretended to be oblivious to their flirting.

The wagon ride was bumpy. They rode all the way down the main street, turning right after passing the last store. One of those salt storage sheds was ahead. It looked like a pyramid.

"There it is," said Draven.

"Road salt?" asked Luanna. "I don't get it."

Draven hopped down from the wagon, grabbing a crowbar before heading to the oversized doors of the building. All three of them followed behind him. Ashley was curious what he was up to, and obviously Luke and Luanna were, too.

"When things started going to shit, some people were ahead of the game. They prepared, stockpiled, hoarded supplies. Most of them didn't make it, but what they left behind has proved a benefit to us. It's just a matter of finding the goods."

Draven bashed the lock off the door, the metal clanging until it broke apart. He took a breath and stepped back, stretching out his arm in greeting.

"Go ahead."

Luke opened the doors. Ashley and Luanna peered into the dark space as the sunlight filtered into the room.

"Oh my God," Luanna whispered.

Ashley covered her mouth with both hands. The salt storage was filled with food—boxes, sacks, and containers full. She began to cry, hot tears streaking down her cheeks. Food supplies meant they wouldn't have to worry or venture out into the world for a very long time. It felt like a miracle.

Chapter Nine

With careful planning, Draven knew they were going to be well set for the next two years. Not only did they have canned food, but also seeds ready to get started on planting. Luanna surprised him by revealing she was once a keen gardener and was more than happy to take the lead on growing crops and doing what needed to be done to ensure their kingdom survived.

He put her in charge of that and made sure she had everyone at her disposal to prepare, plant, and plan all the necessary items she'd need to keep them all well fed. She thrived with purpose, and now she had it.

Glancing across the field, he gritted his teeth. Ashley knelt down in the dirt. Her long hair was pulled back into a baseball cap, one from his room, and she was getting her hands dirty. Just yesterday she admitted to him she'd not gotten her period, so they were waiting another couple days for her to take the test. He needed to know if she was pregnant with his child.

Running fingers through his hair, he felt ready to punch someone for allowing her outside. Since the attack, he'd granted her more freedom. Of course, Luanna had also proven herself to be a fierce protector, which was another reason he didn't have a problem with her being around the others.

The men knew to keep their hands off. Ashley belonged to him, and no one else. He didn't fucking share.

Storming across the field, he ignored the greetings he was getting. Hands on his hips, he glared down at her, stepping directly into her light so she couldn't see.

"Hey, you're in the way." She sat back on her knees and looked up at him. "Oh, hey you," she said, offering him the sweet, sexy smile he absolutely loved but didn't want to get involved with right now.

"What the hell are you doing?"

"I'm helping. What does it look like I'm doing?" she asked, dusting her hands off as she did so.

"You're not supposed to be out here, messing around in the dirt."

"Draven, I want to do my bit to help. I like messing around in the dirt." She reached down, picking up a handful of soil and letting it fall through her fingers. "See, fun."

He crouched down, reaching out to cup her cheek. "Babe, I want you back in the house. You're doing too much."

"Draven, I was locked up for a short time because of this stupid thing." She held up her wrist. "You kept me locked up because of your men. We're all finding our way now. Please, don't take this from me. I want to help. We're all a family. I want to be part of this." She cupped his hand, and he saw the sadness in her eyes.

"I'm not going to lock you back up even though I want to. I've got to protect you, always." He slowly slid his fingers down her body. He wanted to linger on her tits, but he didn't. Cupping her stomach, he looked at her. "You could be pregnant."

Again, she covered his hand with her own. "And if I'm pregnant, I'll still be out here attending plants. Everyone is doing something. Pregnancy does not mean incapable."

"Women can get sick."

"I'm going to be doing exactly what I do now until I'm close to giving birth. Unless I'm not capable of doing it."

"You're pregnant?" Luanna asked, coming to stand beside them. She held a chart in her hand, and

Draven saw the concern in the other woman's face.

"She could be."

"What he said. It's not official. I've skipped my period. It happens. We don't know if I'm pregnant yet."

"I've been doing a lot to make sure you get pregnant."

Ashley growled. "Please tell the insane man, I can do my chores here and have a healthy pregnancy."

Luanna held her hands up. "I don't know anything about pregnancy."

"So I can send her in?"

"I know about pregnancy," a man said, coming toward them. He was one of the latest recruits, and Draven knew he was once a doctor. The man had been thorough showing off all of his documentation at the gate. He wanted to survive, to live, and to be useful.

Draven readily accepted him, knowing his skills could come in useful, especially for Ashley.

"Really, what do you know?"

"You can continue to work, so long as you're healthy. Have you taken a test?"

"No."

"Then it's something we need to consider doing right away. She'll need to take folic acid, as well. I'll have to check the medical supplies."

"We emptied out a pharmacy on our last raid," Draven said.

"The name's Miller. If you would allow me to, I'd love to be able to help your woman," he said.

Ashley smiled as she glanced over at him, and he knew she thought she'd won. They were just getting started.

Bending down, he lifted Ashley over his shoulder, being careful in case she was pregnant.

"Draven, put me down."

"We're going to see if we've got any of those tests," Draven said, rubbing his hand over her curvy ass.

"Damn it, I thought we were going to wait."

"I changed my mind. The sooner we know, the sooner we can make sure this is going to be a healthy baby."

Several of his men burst out laughing as he passed. Ashley stopped wriggling on his shoulder, and he mourned the loss of her fight. Entering the house, he took her straight toward the storage of the medical supplies. Miller and Luanna had followed them.

"See if you can find what you're looking for," he said, pointing to the assortment of medicines. Draven found the pregnancy test and held it up for her to see. "We're going to find out if we've been lucky or not."

Ashley didn't make it easy, so he had no choice but to carry her to a bathroom.

Opening up the test, he held it out to her. "Come on, baby, it's not that hard. You pee on this piece here."

"Draven ... I'm scared."

"You've got nothing to be afraid of."

"But what if it says no?"

"Do you want it to say no?"

She shook her head.

"It's not going to say no."

"But what if it does and the doctors got it all wrong? I'm not fertile. Would you still want me?" She pulled away from him, holding her hands up as if to ward him off.

Draven stared at her, a little shocked. "You think I only want you because ... you're fertile?"

"It's the truth."

Draven rubbed at his eyes. "I did when you first arrived here, Ashley. But not anymore and not for a long time. If anything, I've been worried that I won't be able to get *you* pregnant."

He saw tears in her eyes and wondered if she was struggling with her hormones already. He wasn't used to having to deal with hormonal women. He ran his fingers through his hair and released a breath.

"I just … I don't want to disappoint you."

He put down the test, cupping her face. "There's no way on this earth you could ever disappoint me. Fuck, when you first arrived here, I wanted you because you were fertile, but that changed. You changed me. I don't just want you because of your body. I want so much more, and I know only you can give it to me."

"What do you want?" she asked.

"All of you. Every single part of you, and I don't want you to hold back from me. Not ever." He couldn't resist taking possession of her lips, and as he slammed his down on hers, he felt her relent to him. All he wanted to do was show her how he felt. Draven was a soldier, a warrior, and he wasn't good with flowery words or expressing himself. There was no doubt in his mind that he loved her and would always love her. Breaking off from the kiss, he stroked her cheek, watching as she licked her lips. "Ashley, I love you. I fell in love with you against all the odds. Not because you're going to have my baby, but because after all you'd gone through, it didn't stop you from fighting nor did you lose your sweetness. You're everything I've ever wanted in a woman and in my life. I can't give you up. I won't. I want this to be a safe haven for you and for our children. I will fight until my last dying breath to make you happy. To protect you. You own my heart, all of it. This is all yours."

The tears in her eyes started to fall. "You mean it?"

"How can you doubt it? I'm right here, with you.

I'll always be here. I'm the kind of guy who makes everyone pull their weight around here, but with you, I let you take a break."

She chuckled.

"Do you believe me?"

"Yes. I mean, I should know. I'm sorry. I'm just feeling all over the place. Luanna told me I planted some of the seeding potatoes wrong, and I burst into tears. I'm not usually this emotional." He watched her take a breath. "I think we both know what it means though, don't we? For me to be this emotional."

"I'm ready to find out," he said. "Together." Locking their fingers together, with his free hand, he grabbed the test again.

"Let's do this."

****

Pregnant!

The test confirmed it, and Ashley stared at the stick even after six hours of originally peeing on the test. The doctors hadn't been wrong about her. This was unprecedented. A child would be born in their crazy new world.

She sat in the library, legs crossed, staring at the test, feeling a little sick, consumed with worry, and with a real craving for chocolate mint ice cream. She could dream.

Biting her lip, she tried to think of everything and anything to keep her mind out of panic mode.

This wasn't the end of the world. Women had been having babies since the beginning of time. Pioneers had much less than they did now, and they did fine, too.

Draven was excited about it. He announced it for all to hear, and throughout dinner, she had people hugging her, touching her stomach, congratulating her.

"I thought I'd find you here," Luanna said. "I

know you can't have wine or anything, but I got you some soda to celebrate."

Ashley smiled. "I wish I could have had the wine."

Luanna placed a hand on her wrist. "You're still looking at that thing?"

"I'm waiting to see if it will change back." She put the test down on the coffee table, beside Luanna.

"Come on, talk to me. What's going on?" Luanna asked. "This isn't like you. I can see you're stressing out, and it's not good for you or the baby."

She rolled her eyes; she couldn't help it.

"You're worried?" Luanna asked.

"Yes. No. Of course not. What do I have to be worried about? It's all fine. Of course, it's all fine."

Luanna took both of her hands. "I'm not just anyone. I can see you're stressing. Talk to me."

Staring down at her friend's hands, she sighed. "What if I'm not cut out for this?"

"In what way?"

"Being a mother? Half of the world population is gone. Women like me, we're … different. I don't know. I never thought I'd get pregnant."

"You always figured the doctors were lying?"

"Yes." Ashley pulled away from her friend. "I must sound awful."

"No. You sound like a woman who is trying not to freak out and failing."

Ashley groaned. "I should be ready for this. Repopulating the planet and all that. Why am I terrified?"

"Before you, you don't think women were scared?"

"They were?"

"Absolutely. Of course, they were. Why wouldn't

they be? They're bringing in another life, and babies have the way of complicating everything. Especially in the old world. Marriages, relationships, quite a few were set up purely because a baby was involved." Luanna touched her stomach. "You have a gift."

"I feel so guilty." She swiped at the tears. "What if I'm a bad mom?"

"I won't let you. We're all in this together."

She let out a sigh. "I'm sorry. I shouldn't be talking about this."

"You should totally be talking about this. I think you need to talk to Draven. It's his child as well, and you both have to be in this together." Luanna squeezed her hand. "You will always have me and everyone here. We all love and care for you. We all want to help bring this baby into the world. You're going to have so much love and support, you'll be begging for some space."

Ashley smiled. Her fears hadn't disappeared.

"I've got to head back. You're going to be okay?"

"Yeah, of course. I'm totally fine. You know me." She waved her hand in the air in an attempt to ward off her friend's concern.

Luanna kissed her head, leaving her alone.

Leaning her head back on the sofa, Ashley closed her eyes. What if she was the worst mother in the world?

"You're going to be the best mother in the world."

She gasped, turning to see Draven standing near the back of the library. She hadn't heard him come in.

"Draven," she said.

He walked around the furniture, moving to sit beside her. Without asking for permission, he pulled her into his arms. "You're scared?"

It was on the tip of her tongue to lie to him. Staring into his eyes, she knew it would be a mistake.

"I've never been so afraid of anything else in my life. I want to have this baby with you so much." She rested his hands on her stomach, and she closed her eyes, feeling him surround her. Whenever he did this, she felt safe, warm, whole. He was the only one to ever make her feel this way, and she didn't want to lose it. Not him, not ever again. "What makes you think I'm going to be a good mom?" she asked. "We don't know what it's going to be like having a child here?"

He kissed her neck as he chuckled. "I guess, I know you. I know how good and pure you are. I've watched you with the others here. You're sweet and kind. Considerate. I also believe you've got what it takes to mother our child."

"Why am I so afraid?"

"It's new. We're in a war zone. There's no getting away from what we're all fighting. I have no doubt we're going to encounter men and women who want to take from us, but I'm not going to let them." He took hold of her hands in his. "Relax, Ashley. You don't have to fight anymore."

Leaning back against him, she released a breath.

"You know what I see?" he asked.

"What?"

"I see the summer time when our son or daughter is, like, five. They're laughing and giggling as we run around the apple tree. The one just out near the orchard. It has some delicious apples, and I can see us all there, having a picnic from food we've harvested."

"You see a future."

"I see *our* future together. This world, it's shit, I'm not going to lie to you. You're never going to be able to walk down the street alone, nor will you walk with our children to school to meet other kids. No sleepovers, no baby classes. Nothing. We're going to have each other, and the men and women who choose to settle here."

She opened her eyes. The picture he painted was both sweet and sad. Moving out of his arms, she straddled his body, wrapping her arms around his neck. His hands moved to grab her butt, gripping her tightly.

"I love you like this," he said, thrusting his cock up against her. She was surprised to feel him hard already.

"Do you ever think of anything else?"

"When I'm with you, nothing." He rocked against her, and she couldn't help but smile. "I know you don't see it right now, but it's going to be okay."

"You can't predict the future."

"I know, but I can make sure you're taken care of. I love you, Ashley. My love for you will never change, and I'm going to make sure you will laugh and smile at every single turn." He slid his hands up her body, going to her tits. He cupped them, and his thumbs gently caressed over her erect nipples. "They're going to be so full and ripe soon, to feed our child."

She moaned, biting her lip as he pinched the hardened buds.

"Draven?"

"Have you stopped worrying yet?"

"No."

His hands moved to her skirt, and he began to pull it up her body. She didn't fight him.

"I would marry you if I could, Ashley. You're my wife in all the ways it matters, and I will never let you go, never give you up, and I'm going to show you time and time again, just how much I love you." He moved quickly, pushing her to the sofa. He lifted her hands above her head.

"What are you doing?"

"I'm going to make sure you relax." He opened

her shirt, and his lips began to trail down her body, going to her left tit, then her right. He sucked on each beaded nipple before gliding down her stomach, making her moan as he worked.

Her body belonged to him, as did her heart and her soul. Even with the world around them falling apart, she knew in Draven's arms, she would be safe. Forever.

She cried out as he spread open the lips of her pussy and his tongue began to tease her slit.

"Watch me taste you, Ashley. Just feel and see everything I'm doing to you."

She stared at him as he sucked her clit into his mouth. It was next to impossible to keep her eyes open when all she wanted to do was let go, to find her orgasm.

Draven was the one in charge, and even though she had fought him in the beginning, she loved him being the man of the house. The one in charge. The one who would always have the final say.

She sank her fingers into his hair, rocking her hips against his face, pressing her pussy against him, not wanting him to let go.

"That's it, baby. Let me taste you. Let me make you feel so good." His hands cupped both of her breasts as his tongue glided down to fuck inside her. It felt so good, she couldn't stand the pleasure. It was so intense.

Draven knew how to hit the right spot inside her, and it drove her need higher.

She screamed his name, the sound echoing around the room. She hoped no one came in as he took her, showing her just how good he could be.

"Come for me, Ashley. Let me see you let go."

She did, crying his name once again. Draven teased her pussy, driving her over the edge, and slowly brought her down.

Her mouth was dry, and she couldn't think a

coherent thought.

"It's not possible for you to be bad at anything," he said.

"How can you be so sure?"

"You're the love of my life, and I know you'll always be the best for me, for our child, and for our people." He gripped the back of her neck as he kissed her hard. She tasted herself on his lips, but it didn't repulse her.

"What about you?" she asked.

"This wasn't for me. This was for you." He got up off the sofa, and she let out a squeal as he picked her up. "You can take care of me later."

Chapter Ten

10 months later

"How long do we have?" asked Draven.

"No more than twenty minutes until they're at the gates," said Luke.

They were on the roof, the highest vantage point of the kingdom. Luke was on his stomach with the binoculars in hand. A horde of men and a few vehicles were heading their way. Draven had never seen such a large, sophisticated group pass through before. They moved boldly, not even attempting to sneak up on them. A trickle of fear left him unsettled. He had a lot to lose.

"We'll arm all the men. Get the women to safety," said Draven. "There may be more of them than us, but I'll die before I let them through the gates."

Luke lowered the binoculars, glancing up at him. "Let's hope it doesn't come to that. I like to think positive before assuming they're coming to destroy us."

"Has anyone come through here with good intentions before?"

"Ashley?"

Draven scowled. "That was different. She was running from men like those."

"Again, you're assuming they're the enemy."

Draven started to climb down from the roof. "Let's agree to hope for the best and prepare for the worst. Get to the weapons locker."

Luke nodded.

It had been almost a year since they'd started expanding their walls and growing more crops. They were overflowing with abundance, and he thought things couldn't get better. Now there was a risk of losing everything. If the large group of vandals pillaged their crops and food stores, they'd be back to square one again. Forced to travel in search of supplies, never knowing if they'd survive one day to the next.

And they could lose a lot more than their crops.

Draven ran a hand through his hair as he walked through the courtyard. Luanna jogged up to him.

"Tell me what's going on," she said.

"Nothing to worry about." He kept walking, trying to ignore her.

"Don't bullshit me, Draven. You look like you've seen a ghost, and Luke's been on the roof all morning. What's coming?"

He stared down at her. "Trouble. Looks like two dozen men and vehicles."

"Shit," she said.

"Luke's going to distribute weapons soon. We need to keep the others safe."

She nodded. "The weapons lockers are the most secure. They're fortified. We should bring the old and young there."

"Agreed," he said. She rushed off, keeping quiet as she passed other people. Luanna had become an asset. When she first arrived with Ashley, he'd wanted her gone. Now Draven couldn't imagine life without her underfoot. Luke would agree, considering they'd been dating for months.

So much hope had been seeded since Ashley came into his life. Morale was at an all-time high, and their independence had never been stronger thanks to their hard work and planning.

Now everything could be in jeopardy.

He found Ashley in the gardens. She was sewing something. The last thing he wanted to do was make her afraid or insecure. Every fiber of his being wanted to keep her happy and safe.

"What're you making?" he asked.

She looked up at him, the sunlight making her squint. "We don't have any baby clothes, so I'm making some myself. It's not too hard."

"That's very industrious."

Ashley raised an eyebrow. "Industrious?"

Draven shrugged, squatting down to her level. "Where's the baby?"

"Napping."

Their daughter just turned three months old. Clara was perfectly healthy, and they had no reason to believe she'd be infertile. Humanity would survive. They'd survive.

"Before you came all I worried about was staying alive. Death terrified me because once I was gone, that would be it. You changed all that, gave me something bigger to live for."

She smiled, her blue eyes bright in the sunlight.

"Thank you for giving me a beautiful daughter," he said. "For showing me what real love is—"

"Something's wrong, Draven. What is it?"

"It's all the truth."

She set down her sewing, twisting to face him. "I know you better than this. You're worried about something."

Was he that easy to read? All he knew was he couldn't lie to her.

"It's probably nothing. Luke isn't even worried."

"About?"

"There's a group of men heading our way. Luanna's already rounding up the vulnerable as a precaution."

"Just men?"

He nodded.

"I doubt they're looking for sanctuary then. And you're worried, which means this could end badly."

"I won't let them hurt you or Clara. No way in hell will anyone get their hands on either of you."

"I'm only worried about our baby." She stood up and paced. "I'm not as helpless as you think, Draven. I'd die to protect her."

"You're the best mother, baby." He wrapped his arms around her, holding her still. Draven kissed her forehead. "You make me so proud every day—"

"Where's the safest place?" she interrupted.

He shrugged. "The weapons lockers are fortified. That's where Luanna's taking the old and young."

She shook her head. "I'd feel safer at a higher vantage point. I'll stay with Clara in our room. Anyone who comes through the door will be in for a surprise."

He'd been training her in various weapons during her pregnancy. It was better to be safe than sorry, especially after being hijacked on their last town run. It was one thing to point a gun, but it was another to know how to use it properly under stress.

"No one will come through the door," he said.

It was a promise he intended to keep.

A fertile woman and a baby born after the virus would be valuable commodities in their fucked-up world. He didn't intend to share or hand either of them over.

She rose up on her tiptoes and kissed him. He closed his eyes, savoring the feel of her lips and light brush of her tongue. "I'll get the baby."

"Remember, just a precaution," he said, hoping Luke was right.

Ashley nodded, then picked up her sewing as she left the gardens. He stayed rooted in place for a while, looking around at their crops and the flowers that were flourishing along the walls. Survival had turned into paradise, and he didn't want to lose it.

"Boss!"

Draven snapped out of his reverie and looked toward Luke. How much time had passed since he'd climbed down from the roof? He jogged over to the courtyard to meet his friend and the other men. They were all armed. Benjamin tossed him a shotgun. He caught it in both hands, then used the strap to sling it over his shoulder.

"They're only a couple minutes away," said Luke.

He took the binoculars and used an opening in the gate to see what was coming. A heavy-duty truck with a covered back—there could be a lot more men hiding. It crawled along with a couple pick-up trucks, dust billowing behind them. He tried to focus in on the faces of the men, but the dust and movement obscured his vision.

"How many do you think that truck could hold?" he asked Luke.

"What if it's women and children?"

Draven shook his head. Who'd cart around their families … unless they were desperate. Desperate men were more dangerous than common vandals.

"We have the advantage," said Benjamin. "They're outside the walls. As long as we maintain our perimeter, they won't be able to take us."

"I say we fuck them before they fuck us," said Ian. Much of the mob agreed, raising their weapons and chanting. As tempted as Draven was to engage in their energy, he had to keep a level head as leader.

"First, we talk!" he shouted, settling down the crowd. "If that doesn't work…"

"Yeah, let's hear what they have to say. They could just be passing through," said Luke."

Benjamin laughed without humor. "You see the armed vehicles they have? Some of them are in uniforms.

They mean business, which means it won't end up well for any of us if we don't act soon."

"They're almost here," said Draven. He could see them without binoculars now, hear the engine, and the murmur of distant voices. His heart raced. Was Ashley safely upstairs with their baby? Would they be able to keep the strangers out? He had a handful of skilled men, but the rest were regular civilians with no experience with violence.

He'd built this kingdom from nothing. Draven had no plans on handing it over.

****

Ashley settled the baby in her bassinette and then leaned out the window to watch the outsiders approach the gates. She had a clear view of the courtyard from her vantage point. Things were so much different now. If men broke into her room, it wouldn't just be her life at stake. She had an innocent baby to consider now. Her defenses flared inside her. Nobody was going to take her Clara.

"What's your business here?" asked Draven. The voices drifted upwards, allowing her to hear the conversation that could be the beginning of a nightmare.

She could feel the tension in their air, like the weight of humidity, making it difficult to breathe.

"How many souls do you have inside?"

Draven crossed his arms over his chest. "That's not your concern, is it? What the fuck do you want?"

Everyone was still and quiet. Then the stranger smiled.

"We're from the city to the east. We're one of seven groups dispatched to find survivors. To spread the good news."

"Good news?"

Ashley left the window and rushed over to the

balcony to get closer to the conversation.

"We're taking the world back, trying to undo the damage from the virus. We have a cure. More than enough for every fertile behind your walls. There's food, medical care, and other resources set up in the major cities, if you're in need. We're trying to get the word out."

A few other men opened a tarp door on the side of the truck, and two of them carried out wooden crates, small glass bottles clanking inside.

"What's in the crates?" asked Luke.

"One vial now, one in two weeks. That's all it takes. If you've survived this long, you have natural immunities, but the next generation will need protection. Any fertiles should take it. The most important thing is we're getting control over the chaos. With the cure and the coordinating we've been doing, things are only going to get better."

"You won't be insulted if we don't take your word for it," said Draven.

A rush of fear ran turned Ashley's blood cold. Was her baby in danger?

The man put up his arms as the other two set down the crates in front of the gates. "Just passing through, spreading the good news. The services in the city are open to anyone. It's time we have peace again, don't you agree?"

Ashley waited for Draven's reaction. In fact, all the men looked to him for the next move. If what these travelers said was true, it would mean they wouldn't have to live with so much fear of the unknown. It would mean Clara would be safe.

"How do we know that's not poison? Once we're all dead, you break in and take over."

"I thought you'd say that." The man nodded to

one of the men who'd carried the crates. He pried it open with a crowbar and stepped back. "Pick a bottle."

Draven reached through the bars of the gates and lifted a random vial. They all watched as the stranger took it, popped the cap, and swallowed it in one long gulp.

"You've never taken it?" asked Luke.

"Oh, I've taken it, but one more won't kill me. I was on your side of the wall not long ago, so I understand exactly why you're not ready to trust. Be sure to give it to any fertile women passing through."

"Where will you go now?" Draven asked.

"We'll keep on our course, looking for more settlements and travellers. We have to stick together. That's what humanity is all about."

Draven nodded, but didn't move.

The men started to close the flap on their truck, preparing to leave. Then Clara started crying. It seemed that very moment was void of sound, not a breath or a whisper. Everyone looked up to the balcony where she stood. Ashley wanted to rush inside, but her feet stayed rooted in place.

"A baby?"

Would things change now? Would their true natures make their appearance? She held her breath, hoping this wasn't a major con job.

"You've never heard a baby cry?" asked Draven. She knew he was trying to replicate disinterest, but he had to be as terrified as she was.

"Not out here. How many fertile females do you have?" asked the stranger.

"I don't see how that matters."

"If the mother hasn't received the cure, the baby needs to have it as soon as possible. We're looking to the future now, but it won't be easy to rebuild. It will take generations."

"You're right. It will." Draven palmed his rifle. A subtle threat.

The stranger nodded, stepping back. "You're a lucky man. Take care of her. The world won't rebuild itself."

Then they were gone, packing up and driving off in the direction they were heading. Time seemed to halt until even the dust in the distance settled, signaling the convoy was gone.

Only minutes later, there was a knock on the bedroom door, making her gasp.

"Draven?"

"It's me, baby. Open up."

She removed the barricades she'd put in place and unlocked the door. Draven stood there, the same large imposing man she'd fallen in love with. It felt like a lifetime ago since she first arrived at his kingdom.

"Do you believe them?" she asked.

He still hadn't moved. "What else do we have but hope? They're gone now. If everything he said is true, that means our threat level will drop and keep dropping. Clara will be safe."

"But we don't let down our guard," she said.

Draven smirked. "No, little one, we always have to be ready." He strode in, step by step, pushing the door shut as he entered.

He looked hungry.

She backed up, intimidated by his sexual energy, but not afraid. He looked worn and tired, a man pushed to the limits of stress. And he wanted her.

Just knowing what he was thinking made her pussy pulse.

"Ever since Clara was born, you've been hiding yourself from me. Why?"

She kept moving back, reaching behind her for something to anchor her. "A baby changes a woman's body. You might not like what you see."

Even before having her first child, she'd been a big, curvy girl. Everything was only exaggerated since giving birth. She couldn't bear the thought of Draven becoming unattracted to her, especially when he continued to turn her on effortlessly.

Draven scowled. "You have no idea how much you turn me on, Ash. Your big tits, heavy and full of milk. Your nipples swollen and pink. I want to get my hands on every soft curve. You're all woman, and there's not a minute of the day I'm not fantasizing of getting you naked."

"You're not just saying that, are you?"

He growled. "I've been patient, but it's been over three months. I think you've had more than enough time to heal up from having Clara, no?"

She paused, then gave the slightest nod. Her body had healed over a month ago. It had been her insecurities keeping her from giving in to their mutual desire.

"Let me see you."

"Please, Draven, no."

"You weren't so shy before. That shouldn't change now. I'm going to prove just how fucking desperate I am for you, baby." He ran his hand through her hair, and she closed her eyes, savoring the simple intimacy. She needed so much more.

Ashley pulled off her shirt, setting it on the low dresser she'd been leaning against. "There, does that make you happy?" She'd been braless under her shirt. Her tits were huge and cumbersome since her milk came in, and she couldn't imagine any man finding them attractive. "They're not cute and perky. Not that they ever were."

"You're trying my patience again, Ashley. Don't put yourself down. You're my queen, my everything, and I won't have it. Understand?"

She shrugged.

"They say every man has a fetish, whether he admits it or realizes it himself. Me, I love big, soft tits I can drown in and hips I grab and hang on to while I fuck you. When you walk, that little bounce makes my dick hard every time."

He squeezed her breasts together, and she saw his jaw tighten. A drop of milk slipped out, and she cringed. "I'm sorry."

"For what? Being the mother to our child?" He licked his lips. "I swear I've died and gone to heaven. You're so fucking sexy, I still can't believe you're all mine."

He began to push down her skirt, and she didn't stop him as it slipped over her hips and pooled at her feet. Draven bent down and shimmied her panties down, smoothing his hands back up her thighs once she was completely nude.

"Draven…"

"What is it, baby? Want to refuse me again? The only thing I want to hear coming out of your mouth is you begging me to fuck you." He cupped her face in both hands, looking at her with such intensity her breath caught. "You say you're insecure? How do you think *I* feel when the woman I love avoids making love to me like I'm her enemy?"

Was that really how he felt?

A wave of guilt took her by surprise. Nothing was more attractive to her than Draven. Watching him work out day in, day out, in nothing more than gym shorts was torture. Sleeping next to his hard, muscled body at night while keeping her hands to herself hadn't been easy. She craved him, desired him as she always had. Her own foolish thoughts had kept her away.

"You're not my enemy," she whispered. "I love you, your body, and making love to you. I never meant to hurt you."

"Let's put the past aside and start from right now. Our new beginning," he said. Draven ran his hands over the curves of her hips. "Now, will you let me touch you? Will you stop pushing me away?"

"How about we start with a kiss?"

He smirked and moved in immediately, his tongue seeking entrance as he devoured her mouth with his. He dominated her, making her feel spineless in his arms. The soul-deep connection, the intimacy—it was exactly what she'd been missing all these months. She didn't realize how starved for affection she was.

His hands were all over her, squeezing and teasing as he kissed down her neck, teasing her pulse points. "Oh God, I've missed this," he said.

He sounded feral, a man on the edge, and she loved the fact he was desperate for her.

"You want to make love to me?"

"Maybe tomorrow. Right now, I'm going to fuck you," he said.

She couldn't contain the little moan that escaped. It sounded as needy as she felt. "Yes, Draven."

"I love it when you're a good girl. Never push me away again. I don't think I could take it."

"I'm yours. I've never loved another man."

He hoisted her onto the dresser top, then undressed in front of her. His biceps bulged as he unfastened his belt. When he slipped out of his pants, his cock sprang up, hard and virile. She knew exactly how good it felt to be ravaged by him.

"Open your legs."

She loved when he ordered her, taking control during sex. There was something uniquely erotic about it. Ashley did as told, opening herself up for him.

"Was that so hard, baby?" He pressed two fingers into her cunt as he kissed her hard on the mouth. He slowly finger-fucked her, and she drenched his fingers. She thought she'd come right on the dresser top she was wound so tight.

Before she knew it, he replaced his fingers with his thick cock. She braced herself, knowing exactly how pent up her man was. She exhaled on a moan as he filled her. The satisfaction swelled within her, a wash of heat and fullness overwhelming her senses.

"Do you like that?" he asked.

"I love it."

"Then I'll give you more." Draven held her hips and began to fuck her, pistoning in and out of her pussy with his rock-hard erection.

It felt so good, so damn addictive. Soon, she was soaring. Why had she denied them when they were so good together?

Draven rammed into her like an animal. She held his shoulders, her fingers exploring the muscles of his arms and back as he brought her closer and closer to orgasm. Ashley could feel it blossoming deep in her womb, a pressure and heat that would leave her screaming.

"You're still nice and tight, baby. You feel perfect around my cock."

They kissed, the fucking merging with their love for each other. It was perfect, powerful, and she couldn't hold back another second. Her orgasm detonated, her core making her entire body quiver as waves of contractions milked Draven's cock.

He groaned, joining her in that beautiful sweet

zone.

His back was slick with clean sweat, his breathing slowly settling. "I'm sorry, Ash. Our first time since the baby should have been special."

He helped her slip off the dresser to her feet. "Three months is a long time. I'm not surprised we didn't make it to the bed." She smiled up at him.

"You're amazing, you know that, right?"

Ashley rested her head to his chest. He ran his fingers through her hair. "I want to be a good wife to you, and a good mother to Clara. I'm learning as I go."

"You're perfect, baby. You make me proud every day. This life isn't a fairy tale, but as long as I'm with you, I wouldn't change a thing."

"I'm so glad Luanna brought us here. You've chased away all my fears and showed me what unconditional love really is," said Ashley.

"A king is nothing without his queen. I understand that now."

He kissed her on the lips. A soft kiss. A kiss full of promises.

They may not know what the future held for them, but they'd survive it together. As a family.

The End

www.samcrescent.com

www.staceyespino.com

SAM CRESCENT AND STACEY ESPINO

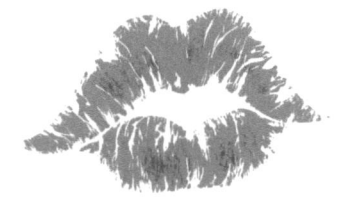

EVERNIGHT PUBLISHING ®

www.evernightpublishing.com